"As I read *Diary*…I felt as if I had been gi[...] [...]ing into the life and heart of Caitlin O'Conne[...] [...]derful and mysterious ride as we are allowed a rare chance to travel alongside a teenage girl as she lives in the real world. This is a unique and refreshing read—fun and entertaining, while at the same time moving and insightful. Read and learn."

"Creative and impactful! The *Diary* drew me in as my concern for Caitlin and her friends grew stronger each page I turned. It gave me the inside story relative to issues I see in my own life—and among my friends and peers. I recommend this book to every teenage girl going through the struggles of peer pressure, dating, and other temptations we face in life."

"As a teacher I found *Diary* to be a realistic look into the lives of Caitlin O'Conner and her friends. This book is dynamic, challenging, and fun!"

"In *Diary of a Teenage Girl,* Melody Carlson captures the voice of teens today in a character we can all relate to. This book sends the message every parent, youth pastor, and wise student wants to share. The unique peer perspective makes it very effective. Integrating the crucial message of the gospel, it forces us to weigh issues and causes us to look at a young person—in reality, ourselves—objectively. It challenges, convicts, and leaves us with hope for the future. I highly recommend this book."

Diary of a Teenage Girl

Becoming Me by Caitlin O'Conner

Melody Carlson

Multnomah®Publishers *Sisters, Oregon*

DIARY OF A TEENAGE GIRL
published by Multnomah Publishers, Inc.

and in association with the literary agency of Sara A. Fortenberry

©2000 by Melody Carlson
International Standard Book Number: 1-57673-735-7

Cover photograph by PhotoDisc / Mel Curtis
Cover design by David Carlson Design

Multnomah is a trademark of Multnomah Publishers, Inc., and is registered in the U.S. Patent and Trademark Office. The colophon is a trademark of Multnomah Publishers, Inc.

Printed in the United States of America

For information:
MULTNOMAH PUBLISHERS, INC.
POST OFFICE BOX 1720
SISTERS, OREGON 97759

Library of Congress Cataloging-in-Publication Data
Carlson, Melody.
   Diary of a teenage girl : Becoming me, by Caitlin O'Conner / by Melody
Carlson.   p. cm.
Summary: Sixteen-year-old Caitlin O'Conner keeps a six-month diary in which she records the day-to-day events of her life as well as her struggles to understand herself and God's plan for her future.
   ISBN 1-57673-735-7 (pbk.)
[1. Diaries—Fiction. 2. Self-perception—Fiction. 3. Interpersonal rela-
tions—Fiction. 4. Christian life—Fiction. 5. High schools—Fiction.
6. Schools—Fiction.] I. Title.
   PZ7.C216637 Di 2000   00-009655
   [Fic]—dc21

00 01 02 03 04 05 06—10 9 8 7 6 5 4 3 2 1 0

ONE

Monday, January 1 (a rather uneventful new year, so far anyway)

I heard somewhere that when you write in a diary you should pretend that you're writing a letter to a really good friend, someone you trust completely, and you know will never laugh at you. So that's what I'm telling myself, because to tell the truth I feel kind of silly writing about my life in this dorky little book. And it's funny because I've actually had this diary for several years now, and suddenly it hits me—like hey, I'm sixteen! According to some people this should be one of the most memorable eras of my whole life. Well, I'm not too sure I even want to remember <u>everything</u> about being sixteen, but on the other hand, things seem to be looking up lately, and it might actually be fun to track how the rest of my junior year goes. Especially considering the first few months have been pretty dull so far.

But first of all, let me say this: Being sixteen is not

really that <u>sweet</u>. And furthermore, it's not terribly exciting either—at least not for <u>me</u> (although I'm certain that some kids my age are having a really great time). Take last night, for instance, I wanted to go to a New Year's Eve party with my friend, Beanie Jacobs. But do you think I got to go? Yeah, right! To protest, I stayed up in my room most of the night, until my mom literally begged me (using her famous it's-a-holiday guilt trip combined with the promise of double-dutch brownies) to "come join the family." And then we watched this really lame video about a bunch of stupid kids who got lost in the woods. And then we stayed up until midnight and watched our neighbors shooting off (what are supposed to be illegal) fireworks. Well, big whoopdee-doo!

But back to being sixteen and how it's not so sweet. What some people don't realize is that sixteen comes with its own set of problems. Like, take driving for instance. I was all excited when I got my license the end of last summer (on my birthday, no less!), and I thought for sure my parents would want to get me a car now. Naturally, I didn't expect a new car (although I wouldn't mind having one of those cool VW Bugs with the little flower vases on the dashboard—maybe in yellow or blue), but I would have settled for almost any old thing with four wheels, as long as it ran decently. But do you think I could get them to spring for a car (even though I patiently explained how they'd never have to haul me around everywhere, and how I would even give my little brother rides to his stupid ball games not to mention run an endless amount of errands for them)? <u>Well, think again!</u> "You don't want to deal with <u>that</u> kind of responsibility yet, Caitlin Renee," Mommy says ever so sweetly. (I'm pretty sure she even patted me on the head!)

Honestly, sometimes my parents treat me like I'm still ten years old! And, of course, they say it's because they love me, but I think the truth is they don't really trust me. They probably think if they give me just the tiniest taste of freedom that I'll run hog-wild, get a tattoo, and start smoking dope or something equally disgusting! Why can't they believe in me—just a little? I mean, I've never given them a single reason <u>not</u> to trust me (at least nothing of any real significance). It's just not fair. About the only thing they willingly let me do is to go to our church's high school youth group functions—and, man, let me tell you, there are some kids in there who are pretty bad news. Not exactly a great "influence" as my dad likes to call any teenage kid he doesn't quite get (take my best friend, Beanie, for instance, but I'll get to her later). Anyway, the thing is, I don't even tell my parents about the kids in youth group who smoke and drink and God only knows what else—or I'd never get to go <u>anywhere</u> until I turned twenty-one!

Now I'll try to say something nice about my parents (just in case they're reading this). <u>And if they are—I will take back every single word of it, and never, ever speak to the old snoops again!</u> Okay, for the most part, my parents are pretty cool (and not the kind of people to read other people's diaries!). For one thing, they've managed to stay married to each other for almost twenty years (a pretty big deal when everyone else's parents seem to be splitting up); and my dad has a pretty interesting job at an advertising firm downtown, while my mom teaches first grade. I guess I could've done worse as far as parents go. Like my best friend, Beanie Jacobs, her dad was a cocaine addict who left her mom with nothing but overdue bills when Beanie was still in diapers. On top of that, her mom's kind of freaky and irresponsible, plus she drinks too much and forgets to pay her bills. I know she got married really young, but it's kind of like she never grew up. But she actually makes Beanie act like the parent most of the time, which is pretty weird, if you ask me.

Of course, the one good thing about that whole Beanie situation is that she gets to do whatever she wants whenever she wants. And I kind of envy that. Oh, sure, I know it has its down side too. Let me tell you, Lynn Jacobs (Beanie's mom) can be pretty scary sometimes, and I've seen her tear into Beanie like she's a dog or something less than human. As a consequence I try to never get on that woman's bad side (which lately seems to be every side). Anyway, Beanie's been my best friend since sixth grade (when we both discovered we were totally hopeless on the violin). I could tell right off she was really smart, and she had this really dry sense of humor. Plus, I liked that she wasn't afraid to speak up and say how she felt (at least around anyone but her mom).

Now, I'll be the first to admit that Beanie Baby (she goes absolutely nuts when I call her that, which I rarely do, except if I'm ticked at her about something) tends to dress, well, shall I say, outlandishly (I've been reading Jane Austen books lately and sometimes I wish we still talked like that)? But back to Beanie and how she has this rather interesting sense of style (you see, her mom never gives her any money for clothes, so she has to come up with all these creative ways of dressing—and she actually shops at Goodwill, and then she even <u>sews</u> some of her weird stuff together). And sometimes she even dyes her hair some pretty wild colors like magenta or midnight blue. Normally it's almost black and very curly which she says is because her dad was Jewish, although she doesn't practice his religion.

But Beanie's pretty fun to hang with, and I'm glad she's my friend. My parents didn't like her at all at first. But then I got her going to youth group with me. And now they think she's okay but strange, and I don't think they quite trust her. Beanie's actually very pretty (in a sultry kind of way) and one time my mom (trying to be helpful) wanted to give her a complete makeover—but that's another story. Let's just suffice it to say that when Mom was done, Beanie looked like a Mary Kay poster child. Poor Beanie.

Well, I guess that's enough for one night. So, now, you can see how my life is just so terribly exciting. Like, wow, maybe they'll make this book into movie some day! <u>Not!</u>

Wednesday, January 3 (back to school)

I need to say that I read back over my first entry in this diary and had to laugh. I mean, I sound like such a blabbermouth. And in real life I'm not even like that. In fact, some people think I'm rather quiet and reserved. My grandma says that's a good thing because there's a Proverb that says something like "even a total fool can appear wise if she keeps her mouth shut." Anyway, I guess the way we express ourselves in writing isn't always the way we express ourselves in real life (and I notice I use a lot of parentheses too). But that's okay—I think writing is fun. Now back to my life...

Okay, today I'm thinking about the pros and cons of popularity (well, mostly the pros). And believe me, I realize (as much as any sixteen-year-old possibly can) that popularity is highly overrated and it's not like it's ever been my primary goal in life. But I guess I never wanted to be a total geek either! And it's not like I am. Not really anyway. Okay, I'm not popular, but I'm not such a loser. I guess I'm just not much of anything. I mean I'm not in any particular group in school—not a geek or a freak, not exactly an academic, and certainly not a jock! Mostly I just hang with Beanie, and <u>sometimes</u> with some of the kids from youth group (but then they can act pretty geeky at times, and we don't always like being connected with them, not that anyone would really care since we are basically nobodies anyway).

But just because we're "nobodies" doesn't mean that kids who think they are "somebody" should put us down. Does it? I mean, I don't think I put other kids down (even if I think they're total geeks), but I suppose if I was being really honest (which was my original goal in this diary, so I better stick to it)...well, I suppose I might act just a little superior sometimes. I mean, it's not like I really think I'm better than anyone else or anything—but I suppose I might act a little bit snooty, especially when I'm afraid that someone else is going to put me down anyway. I know that's not very nice, but it's the truth.

So, back to the question of popularity. I have to admit that when I was a little kid I used to think it'd be so cool to be the most popular girl in the whole school. Like my Aunt Stephie—she's my mom's baby sister, but so much younger she could almost be my big sister. Anyway, I remember how Grandma used to complain that the phone "rang night and day" for Aunt Stephie. She was a cheerleader and had this really cool boyfriend who looked just like Tom Cruise (Tom was more popular back then, although I still think he's pretty cool).

Anyway, all that popularity stuff seemed pretty great to an eight-year-old kid, and I remember thinking that when I was in high school, I wanted to be exactly like Aunt Stephie. Not that her life has turned out all that great as a grownup, at least not according to my grandma (she's always on poor Stephie's case) and I'd have to admit Steph does have some fairly serious problems (like a baby and no husband plus she freeloads baby-sitting from Grandma). So I guess, in some ways, all that popularity didn't do her a whole lot of good in the long run. But just the same, I still sometimes wish that I was one the coolest girls in high school. <u>Now, how's that for honest?</u>

At the same time, I'd like to think that I'm more

mature than that, and I'll admit that Beanie and I sometimes make fun of the "popular" kids (behind their backs, of course!). And like I said, it's not like I'm a complete loser either—in fact, I got my braces off last fall and my skin is almost completely clear now. I got my hair cut in this really cool style during Christmas break, so that it kind of swings back and forth when I walk. And Aunt Stephie said I look just like Gwyneth Paltrow (of course, she wanted me to baby-sit Oliver at the time, and she might've said anything to seal the deal). I've got a magazine with Gwyneth's photo on it, and I studied my face in the mirror, and I do think there is a slight resemblance. And since I got my haircut, it suddenly seems like other people are looking at me differently. Perhaps even some pretty cool people are actually looking my way (unless it's my imagination). But even so, it feels kind of good. I mean all these years before I just felt kind of invisible (which wasn't so bad; I mean, it was better than sticking out in a crowd).

Now I know I must be sounding all lame and desperate to go on like this (not to mention totally shallow); like all I care about is getting some airhead approval from a bunch of kids who aren't all that nice in the first place. And, like I said, it's not like I don't already have any friends. I mean there's always Beanie. There's a few others too. Okay, I admit it, they're mostly from the youth group! But at least I know they'd stick by me through the very worst. I think some of the nicer ones would. I seriously doubt if those popular kids would be like that. Not that

I'll ever have a chance to find out. But on the other hand, I guess I'd be willing to find out, if I had the chance.

Okay, is that so terribly wrong? Is it so wrong to want some _different_ friends for a change? To want life to change and become more exciting? Last week our youth group leader said that if we don't have something that we really think we need, we should pray for it. I wonder if it would be wrong to pray to become popular. I guess the worst that could happen is that God could say no. It might be worth a try. I don't know why God wouldn't want me to have more friends; we're always being told to "reach out" to those around us. Hey, I'm willing to do some reaching here.

Well, all this wondering is probably just a big, stupid waste of time, because I'm sure the popular kids don't want to hang with me anyway. I've heard them make fun of the geeks and nerds and freaks before—as if we're all deaf and can't even hear them. Or maybe they think we have absolutely no feelings at all. In fact, now that I think about it, I can't even believe that I've sat here and actually considered hanging with kids like that in the first place. But I'm supposed to be honest here. And the truth is, I would hang with them if only they would let me. But, I ask you, is that so terribly wrong?

TWO

Thursday, January 4 (a beginning)

Today, Jenny Lambert
talked to me. Now, that might not seem like much to you.
But Jenny is one of the most popular girls in the whole
school. I know, here I go sounding all shallow again. You
know, Jenny is a person too—and I shouldn't hate her just
because she's popular, should I? Besides, for a popular person, Jenny is actually pretty nice. She's friendly and even
though she's a cheerleader, she doesn't seem all that
full of herself the way most of them do. And she's probably the prettiest one of the bunch too. She has brown
eyes and long, dark hair that's shiny and thick. Also, she's
really smart.

She actually spoke to me at the honor society meeting this afternoon (Beanie refuses to join honor society,
even though she's smarter than most of the kids in
there). Honor society is in charge of the Valentine's Day
Dance, and Jenny and I are on the decorating commit-
tee. And while we were compiling our list of what we'll

need (like red and pink crepe paper and stuff) Jenny told me she didn't even want to go to the dance because she had just broken up with her boyfriend, Josh Miller.

Now, if I made a list of all the boys that I'd like to have for my boyfriend, Josh would definitely make the top three. Honestly, he looks just like Matt Damon—same smile, same teeth, everything! But when Jenny ragged on and on about what a total jerk Josh is, I just nodded and agreed with her. I mean, what do I know, just because he's good looking doesn't mean he has any character to speak of.

But the best part was how Jenny even confided in me about him in the first place. And she also told me that she liked my outfit. I got the jeans and top at The Gap last week (with a gift certificate from my other grandma who lives in Pasadena), but my dad thought they were way too expensive—well, I'd say they were well worth it! Then Jenny asked me where I got my hair cut! And she said she wanted to get hers cut like that too. To be honest, at that point, I thought maybe she was just teasing me. You know how kids do that sometimes, saying things like, "Hey, where'd you get those cool shoes?" to some poor kid who's got on a pair of ratty, old Air Jordans or something equally uncool. Anyway, I could tell Jenny wasn't kidding when she actually wrote down the name of the hair salon on her notebook. And the whole time, I just acted really cool and laid back about everything. I never once revealed how totally excited I was just to be talking with her. And then we even walked down to our lockers together!

But now, here comes the embarrassing part. It's something I wouldn't want to tell anyone, but diaries are good for this kind of confession. You see, Beanie spotted me walking with Jenny. One thing I haven't said too much about is how much Beanie just loves to just blurt out all kinds of crazy stuff. She totally gets off on being loud and shocking—mainly to get attention, I think.

Anyway, I was freaking that Beanie was going to say something really stupid about me walking with Jenny, so I tried to avoid making eye contact with her. But as soon as she saw me she said hey just like usual and started coming my way, but then I just turned and looked away from her, pretending like I didn't even know her. I basically just ignored her! I couldn't even believe I did it. For sure, it was totally stupid not to mention risky—I mean, talk about an open invitation for Beanie to really let me have it. But the really weird thing is, <u>she didn't</u>. She just kept on walking by. And now I feel absolutely lousy about the whole thing, and I know I'll have to tell her I'm sorry. I know she will never, in a million years, understand why I'd ever want to be friends with someone like Jenny Lambert. But the truth is, <u>I do!</u> I really do! And it makes me really mad to think that something so simple should suddenly feel so totally complicated.

January 5, Friday (tough choices)

Today, Jenny Lambert invited me to sit with her and her friends at lunch. Beanie, at the time, was nowhere in sight (unbelievable luck!). So I said, "Sure, why not." Man, I thought I must've died and gone to heaven—either that or maybe she was teasing. But no, it was true. And so there I sat with them (Jenny and another cheerleader, both wearing their uniforms, and a couple of her other friends too). The most incredible part was that I didn't make a total fool of myself.

The secret, I've decided, is 1) not to seem overly excited by the whole thing, 2) not to try too hard to impress anyone, and 3) [perhaps most importantly] not to talk too much. But let me tell you, it's a tricky balancing act, at best. I mean, if you're *too* quiet they think you're all stuck up—and that is totally not acceptable when they're the ones who are supposed to be snubbing you. But then if you act all happy and pleased to be with them, they'll treat you like you're part of their little geek outreach program, and for sure that'll be the last time you get to sit at their table. Now don't ask me how I know all this, I think it's like osmosis—like where you just absorb information without knowing it. Or maybe it's because I've been secretly observing them for the past few years. Just like that little kid with her nose pressed up against the candy store window. Pretty pitiful, isn't it? But the good news is—I didn't totally blow it today.

After school, I did get a chance to talk to Beanie about ignoring her yesterday (and I knew by then that she was purposely ignoring me out of pure spite, and maybe hurt feelings too). Of course, my explanation and apology didn't go too well. Just like I thought, she didn't understand at all. She always acts just like she could

care less about who's popular and who's not. At least I
think it's an act—you can never be too sure with Beanie,
she's so dramatic about everything all the time. I must
admit she's one of the best actors in the drama depart-
ment. She's always trying to get me involved, but the
problem is I just freeze up in front of crowds. Maybe I'm
getting better at this acting business now. I mean, look
how cool I can act around Jenny and her friends. In fact,
Beanie should be proud of me. But of course she's not.

Anyway, I told her to give me a break—and that all I
want is to have some more interesting friends. Now that
was the totally wrong thing to say to someone like Beanie.
I know it really hurt her feelings.

"So, I suppose I'm not <u>interesting</u> enough for you?" she
practically screams as we wait for the school bus (yes,
embarrassingly enough, we still ride the school bus). Then
she storms off and sits next to this other girl on the bus
without saying another word to me. (And let me tell you,
it's bad enough riding the school bus, but it's absolutely
the worst when you can't even sit with your friend!) This
is the first time I can remember making her <u>that</u> mad.
But maybe it's a good thing just now. I really do think I
need some space from her—just for the time being.
Besides, Beanie is Beanie, and I'm pretty sure she'll
always be there for me—you know, when I need her.

So, enough about Beanie. Anyway, here's the <u>really</u>
good news. Jenny asked me to go to the mall with her
tomorrow—she's going to get her hair cut almost just like
mine. I don't think I'll have too hard of a time convincing

my parents that Jenny is okay. Especially since her dad is the superintendent of the school district (which sort of makes him my mom's boss). Also, I know they'll respect that Jenny's a cheerleader. My mom was a cheerleader (way back in the dark ages) and I don't know how many times she's nagged at me to try out, but I always refuse. (I say I think it's stupid, but the real reason is I know I'd probably forget every move and, like I said earlier, I'd probably just freeze and make a total fool of myself in front of the entire student body. Thanks, but no thanks!) But anyway, I'm sure Mom will be ecstatic to know that I'm actually hanging with an actual cheerleader.

But here's the best part—Jenny has her very own car! It's a silver Honda Accord, not new, but still in nice condition. It used to be her mom's, but she told me her mom got a brand new BMW (navy blue) for Christmas, and now the Honda is Jenny's! Man, some people get all the breaks! But I'm not complaining, not at all. If I can't have my own car, what's wrong with having a friend with one? I just hope Jenny still likes me after spending a few hours together. And now I have to figure out what I'm going to wear!

January 6, Saturday (breaking the rules)

Okay, you are not going to believe what happened today! First of all, Jenny and I went to the mall just as planned, and we actually had a really great time—but that's not the part you've not going to believe. We saw a couple of Jenny's friends while we were having an Orange Julius at the food court, and so we all just talked and stuff (and, by the way, they both really liked Jenny's new haircut), and anyway, the next thing I know, one of the girls (Heather Larson) invites me to come to her boyfriend's house where he's throwing a birthday party for one of his buddies tonight. I said, "sure, why not," but the whole time I'm freaking out, thinking there's no way my parents will let me go to a party at some boy's house.

But wonder of wonders, they said I could go. Actually, it was my mom who said I could go (my dad was off at his office again—he's been putting in a lot of hours lately). I'm pretty sure the only reason my mom let me go is because she's so impressed with Jenny. I'm pretty certain that if I set both Jenny and Beanie side by side, my mom would pick Jenny to be my best friend (not that Jenny's offering, but she is being pretty nice to me).

So anyway, Jenny picks me up and we drive over to Brian Whittier's house (that's Heather's boyfriend and a fantastic basketball player by the way) where it turns out, Brian's parents are gone for the entire weekend— and I guess it should come as no surprise that, with no parents around, the alcohol is flowing in abundance. I have no idea how Brian got all of it, and of course I don't ask. And even though I feel slightly shocked about the whole thing, I don't let on at all. I just act like everything's cool.

But just the same, I don't consume a single drop of alcohol. The truth is, I'm way too scared. I know for a fact that my parents would kill me if they knew what was going on here, and the whole time I'm looking over my shoulder and worrying that this party's going to get busted big time, and then I'll have a police record, and how in the world would I explain all this to my conservative, church going parents? But what complicates things even further is that everyone at the party is being all cool and chummy to me, and they're all kind of goofy and relaxed (not at all how they act in school), and I'm actually having a pretty good time (other than worrying about getting busted).

So I don't let anyone know that I'm not drinking anything besides club soda. And pretty soon I even start acting all silly like them (like it's contagious or something). Of course, it's a little disturbing (not to mention slightly gross) when a couple of kids get really sick. And one girl throws up all over my favorite shoes—talk about disgusting! But I tell her, "No problem, it's okay." Not that she'll ever remember since she's so totally wasted. I seriously doubt if I'll ever get the smell out of these shoes. But all in all it's not so bad. Not really. But there is one thing that bothers me.

And so now I'm going to be totally honest about something I felt really uncomfortable with tonight—something I totally regret. You see, I let Jenny drive me home even though I knew she was driving under the influence. Of course, she acted like having a few drinks was no big deal, assuring me she was perfectly sober (although I'm pretty sure she wasn't). And I must admit it scared me a lot! Especially when she accidentally drove up over the curb just a block from my house. I mean, my parents have given me all those talks, you know the ones, about how you should never, ever get in a car with a drunk driver. But they never tell you exactly how to avoid it. I really do know it was an incredibly stupid thing to do—and my parents would totally freak if they knew.

I feel pretty guilty about the whole thing, and if anything like that ever happens again, I'll just offer to drive—or maybe I'll just call my parents to pick me up (although that would be unbelievably embarrassing). To be honest, I don't know what I'd do under those same circumstances again. Or maybe I'll just never go to a party like that again. I know how the Bible says to obey your parents. What I did tonight was anything but obedient—still, I didn't drink any alcohol. Now, wouldn't they be pleased about that?

THREE

Wednesday, January 10 (change happens)

Beanie hasn't talked to me all
week. And she wasn't even in youth group on Sunday. I do
feel a little bit bad about that. But on the other hand,
things just keep getting better and better with Jenny
and me. I've eaten lunch with her and her friends every
day so far this week. Although, I must admit it makes me
feel pretty nervous being around them, like I have to act
all perfect and everything—and consequently I can
hardly eat at all, I just sort of pick at my food, which
has caused Heather to suspect that I am slightly
anorexic (which they thought was kind of cool), and I
didn't say anything otherwise, although I'm pretty sure
that I'm not (even if I am a little on the skinny side). I
know that I wouldn't want to be because I saw a movie
once about a girl who died of anorexia and it looked
pretty sick.

Since I've been hanging with the more popular kids, I
spend a lot more time worrying about how I look; how I

talk; what I'm wearing; and all that kind of surface stuff. I mean, I really like hanging with Jenny and her friends, but I'm also afraid it's making me just slightly neurotic. But maybe I'll get used to it, in time. I guess it's the price you have to pay for popularity. I mean, I hear Heather or one of them going on about what a geek some poor girl is, and I know I don't want them saying anything remotely like that about me.

And I have to admit it did bother me when Jessica Taylor (one of the cheerleaders who's not so terribly nice) started picking apart how Beanie dresses while I was sitting with them. She made fun of Beanie's long velvet coat (it's dark brown and I used to think it was one of Beanie's cooler pieces) and then she started calling Beanie a hippie and saying that she's a pothead (which I happen to know is untrue). But did I say anything in Beanie's defense? No way, I was a total wimp.

<u>Sometimes I really hate myself!</u> But it's a dog-eat-dog world out there—what's a girl supposed to do anyway? If I'd stood up for Beanie, I would have been the next one on Jessica Taylor's Hamilton High's Worst Dressed List. And where would that get me? Already, I spend about an hour every night just trying to figure out what I can wear the next day that'll be cool enough to hang with Jenny and her friends without looking like the poor, hopeless misfit of the bunch. I'm telling you, it's just not easy.

But let me tell you just why it's worth it. Remember Brian Whittier (the boy who threw the birthday party last weekend); well, his best friend is Nathan Parker (a really cute guy who is on my top five picks list and a pretty good basketball player too). Anyway, Nathan has been talking and joking around with me this week. Heather said he was asking her all about me—he actually thought I was a new girl who'd moved here from <u>someplace else</u>! Let me tell you, I wish I was from someplace else. It doesn't seem to matter to him that I've only recently begun hanging with Jenny and Heather—he seems to be interested in me for who I am.

The only thing that's bothering me about all this now, is that I'm afraid he'll ask me out, and (now this is really embarrassing) my parents have never let me go out on a date yet. After my dad went to this Christian men's convention a few years ago, he got it into his head that I shouldn't date until I turned EIGHTEEN! Well, at the time, I was only about thirteen and thought my dad was the next thing to God himself, and so I agreed with him (stupid, stupid, stupid!). So, is it fair for parents to hold their kids to some ridiculous promise they made when they were barely entering adolescence? I don't think so!

Anyway, this is not a conversation I'm looking forward to at all. But I intend to have it. I've already started (very subtly) working on my mom, and she seems sort of open to the whole thing. But my mom's been acting kind of strange anyway lately—kind of checked-out or something. It's almost like I can ask her anything and she'll just say "okay, that sounds fine." Not that I mind, but it does bother me a little. Just a little. Anyway, I asked my dad if he would take me to breakfast tomorrow morning—we used to do that a lot; it was our special time together. And he agreed. So tonight I'll sleep with my fingers crossed. And maybe even say a prayer!

January 11, Thursday (get real, Dad!)

Well, I will no longer be considering myself Daddy's little girl. That man is the most narrow minded, suspicious, distrustful person on the entire planet. He sat there in the Denny's booth and told me with a straight face that "high school boys are only looking for one thing!" And, of course, we all know what he means by that. But how ridiculous! Like every single high school guy wants to take out a girl just so he can have sex. I wish my dad would get real!

I mean, I'm not stupid, I know there are a lot of kids doing it (maybe even most kids, the way they talk and all), but not <u>everyone</u>! And why does he think that I would even consider having sex? Just because I'm going out on a date? I mean, think about it, if I wanted to have sex that bad, I could just duck out behind the gym the way I've heard some other girls do—disgusting as that sounds to me. But who does my dad think I am? What have I ever done to make him so distrustful of me that I couldn't go out with a boy and not go to bed with him? Not only that, it really creeps me out to have my dad even thinking that way about me to begin with. I don't know if I want to talk to him again about any of this stuff. And I used to think that Dad and I were so close—sympatico, you know. I think I'd better just talk to my mom instead. Maybe she can turn his paranoid thinking back towards reality. But I doubt that.

Anyway, who am I trying to fool here? Nathan will probably never ask me out. I am planning to go to the basketball game tomorrow since it's at home this week. And if I hang out with Jenny and Heather—well, who knows what might happen after the game? And the best part is, my parents won't stop me from going to a basketball game.

So now the biggest question is: What will I wear? It's not fair that Heather and Jenny get to wear their cheerleader uniforms all the time—just think how many times they don't have to worry about what they're going to wear! Maybe I can get Mom to take me to the mall after school on Friday. I still have some Christmas money left, and besides, she and I haven't done much together lately, not to mention she still needs some softening up just in case the dating question ever arises.

January 12, Friday (twists and turns)

So much has happened in one single day! I almost don't know where to begin. Let's see, first off, Mom and I went to the mall this afternoon. And she was being totally cool about everything. She really likes my new friends, and she even bought me a new jacket and a pair of shoes that were on sale. (I told her my other favorite pair got ruined when I stepped in a mud puddle; okay, so it was a lie, but what was I supposed to say?) Anyway, we ate some pizza at the food court, and then we discussed at length the whole "to date or not to date" situation.

Finally she said she felt it should be <u>my</u> decision (and

I was old enough to make it) and then she promised to talk to Dad about the whole thing. Thank heavens for cool moms! Anyway, then she even waited for me to go into the restroom and put on my new stuff and then she dropped me off at the basketball game. I told her she should've won the coolest mom of the day award, and that seemed to make her happy. Now that I think about it, it doesn't seem like she's been real happy lately. But that's probably just part of being a mom and having to work and stuff like that.

So, anyway, I got to the ball game (looking pretty good, I might add), and I went to sit down in the place where the cheerleaders and everyone sits (right in front), but then I realized the bleachers were already full right there. Then suddenly it hits me—I've never sat with these kids at a game before in my entire life, and just because they're Jenny's friends doesn't guarantee that they'll welcome me with open arms. I didn't know what to do, and I started to turn away, thinking I better go find someplace else to sit, and hoping my face wasn't turning beet red in embarrassment. I even wondered if Beanie might be here somewhere (unlikely as that seemed) and why hadn't I thought this whole thing out better?

But just then, Jenny yelled out, "Hey, Caitlin, there's room for you over here. Scoot over you guys, and let Caitlin squeeze in." And (big sigh) my troubles were over. Thank goodness too, 'cause I don't know what I would've done otherwise. So I sat with all of them during the game, and it was pretty fun, but I couldn't keep my eyes off Nathan, and I'm pretty sure he was looking my way too (at least the few times he was sitting on the bench, which wasn't a whole lot). Then, the game was over (which we won by the way), and Jenny asked if I wanted to go with her over to a little celebration party.

Of course, I agreed, telling myself that if by some chance Jenny should became intoxicated (not that I knew ahead of time that there would be alcohol there), I'd be the designated driver to get us home safely. As we were driving, Jenny confided to me that she'd been missing Josh lately and had devised a plan to get him back.

"But I'll need your help, Cate," she explained (Jenny's the only friend I allow to call me by anything but Caitlin). "Sure, what do you want me to do?" I asked, eager to please. Then she told me that if she could just make Josh jealous, he'd beg her to come back. "But in order to make him jealous," she said, "I need an unattached guy to cozy up to—not just any guy. I mean, he's got to be cute and popular."

Suddenly I know exactly who she means. "Are you thinking of Nathan Parker?" I ask, trying to disguise my shock and disgust. She nods and I feel my insides give a strange little twist. "But Nathan and I aren't even a real couple or anything, Jenny. I mean, I don't really know how I can be of any help to you..."

Well, I'm feeling kind of like a deflated balloon about then.

"That's okay," she continues. "Everyone knows that

Nathan's got his eye on you, Cate. But maybe for tonight, you could just step out of the picture for a little, and let me pretend that he and I are getting together." I'm kind of stunned and don't really know what to say. But how can I say no? And so I just totally wimp out and agree to her plan.

So Nathan and the other basketball players arrive at the party (all happy about tonight's victory), and I just act totally uninterested in him, which really makes me feel completely horrible. I'm wondering, why do people play these kinds of games anyway? And, of course, Jenny steps right in looking all cute and perky in her cheerleader uniform (and that's after she's loosened up with a couple of drinks—I was feeling pretty tempted to "loosen" up myself, but somehow I managed to resist).

And suddenly it seemed like she was all over him, and it actually made me really, really mad. I mean, I <u>thought</u> she was my friend, and I <u>thought</u> it was all just an act to make Josh jealous. But it looked pretty real to me. Finally, I got totally fed up with everything that I just went into another room (it was like a library or office, and I'm pretty sure the kids weren't supposed to be in there, but as usual, the parents weren't home, so who was around to care?). Anyway I sat down in this big leather chair and wondered what in the world I was doing there. And why? And if Jenny was supposed to be my friend, why was she treating me like this? What fun was it to watch a bunch of stupid kids getting totally plastered—and believe me, I felt more like an outsider than ever!

I was just about to pick up the phone and call my parents to come and get me when Josh Miller walked in and asked if he could join me. Not for the first time that night, I tried to conceal my surprise, and said, "Sure, have a seat if you want to join the fun. I'm having a great time." He laughed and sat down. And then we started to talk. It was so weird. Josh Miller and me just sitting in some guy's den and talking. Just a few weeks ago, I never would've dreamed that this could have ever happened—not in a million years!

But there I was, just as cool as anything, carrying on an intelligent and somewhat witty conversation with one of the most popular guys in Harrison High. And a senior too! Josh told me he how didn't really enjoy these drinking parties that much either, saying how most of the kids acted pretty immature and half of them ended up sicker than dogs before the night was over.

Then he said he was going to leave and wondered if I wanted a ride home. I mentioned that I'd come with Jenny, then he said that he thought Jenny was pretty obsessed with Nathan right now and probably wouldn't even miss me. Well that got to me! So, I said, "Sure, why not?" And the two of us walked out to where everyone else was and told them all good-night.

Well, you should've seen the look on Jenny's face! And suddenly I knew I'd blown it big time—and I knew my days of popularity had probably come to a swift end. I guess Josh could sense I was worried when I got all quiet in his car (which was a really nice little Jeep Wrangler, by the way) and he asked me what was wrong. And it was like somebody had uncorked something in me and I ended up just pouring out the whole story about how Jenny had been such a good friend to me, and then how she wanted to make Josh jealous by feigning interest in Nathan, and how I had just totally messed everything up.

Josh ended up just laughing hysterically about the whole thing. And I figured that by now I'd really blown it, and the story would be all over school by Monday, and Caitlin O'Conner (the one week wonder) would be history. But then Josh turned to me and said that he thought I was a really unusual girl and that he wanted to get to know me better. Then he said not to worry about Jenny, that she'd get over it. And if it would help any, he'd talk to her himself. <u>What a guy!</u> Anyway, he dropped me at home, and now he's all I can think about. And now I don't even care if it would make Jenny totally hate me, if I had the chance to go out with Josh Miller I wouldn't think twice. At least I don't think I would...

January 13, Saturday (two strikes)

This afternoon, Jenny calls and she's all just as nice and sweet as you please. So I decide to act kind of indifferent to her, not rude or anything, but just slightly chilly, if you know what I mean. Anyway, it doesn't seem to affect her at all. And finally, she just breaks down and apologizes to <u>me</u>! I'm thinking, this is pretty funny; I leave the party last night with the one guy that Jenny Lambert really likes, and today she's apologizing to <u>me</u>.

So then I told her, quite honestly, that I was sorry too. I explained how I wasn't having much fun last night, and when Josh offered me a ride, I couldn't see any reason not to take it. "I know all about that, Cate," she said reassuringly. "Josh came over this morning and told me the whole story. And I have to thank you—because of what you said, Josh and I are going out again."

Well, as you can imagine, I pretended to be all happy and excited for her, saying how I thought Josh was a pretty nice guy after all and how I hoped that things went better for them this time. (I really hoped that they'd go out on one date and end up in a great big fight and break up for good!)

So now, it looks like I've lost Josh and Nathan all in one stupid weekend. One minute your hopes are flying to the moon and the next minute you've lower than a piece of chewed-up gum sticking to the bottom of someone's dirty sneaker! Being a teenager these days is not for the faint of heart.

FOUR

January 14, Sunday (questions, questions)

I didn't want to go to church today. But naturally I kept this little piece of information to myself. Knowing something about how the mind of a parent works, I felt pretty certain that they'd put two and two together to equal five and thus decide that my new friends (Jenny et al) were a bad influence on me after all. And right now, I'm not too sure about my dad's thinking anyway, so I'm certainly not going to rock the family boat.

So anyway, I got up, got dressed (and believe me there's no need to plan a cool outfit for this crowd) and climbed into the backseat of our Volvo next to my little brother, Benjamin, who became impossible when he turned twelve, and who hasn't bathed (I'd guess by his smell) since last year! Anyway, eager to escape Ben's stench, I leaped out of the car and raced over to the youth house (maybe my dad thought I was excited about going to youth group). To my dismay, Beanie, once again, was not there. Not that I really wanted to hear her lecture me or anything, but suddenly I'm feeling all guilty like if Beanie doesn't go to heaven now, it'll be all my fault. But to tell you the truth, I'm not even sure if I'm going to heaven these days. I mean, just because you go to church doesn't mean you go to heaven. At least that's what our youth pastor said today. And I got to thinking, maybe I'm not going either.

Then here's a really scary thought—what if there is no heaven? I mean, what if all these Christians are working really hard to be so good and perfect (playing by the rules and everything) and come to find out there is no heaven—no hell—just a great big cosmic joke. I have to admit it feels really wrong (is it blasphemy?) to actually write those words down. But the truth is, I'm starting to wonder about all this religious stuff. I mean, for my whole life, it's all I've ever heard, and I guess up until now I've always pretty much believed it. At least I think I did. And even now, despite all this doubtful rambling, I do still believe in God. At least I think I do. But then why am I suddenly feeling so confused about all this stuff? Is it right for me to blindly accept my parents' religion as my own without ever asking any questions for myself? I mean, Beanie's dad is supposedly Jewish, but that doesn't seem to make her Jewish. So what's the deal? So I'm thinking that just because my parents are Christians and go to church (fairly regularly, but not always) that doesn't necessarily mean I have to be like them. Does it? After all, don't we all have to figure these things out for ourselves in the long run?

January 18, Thursday (deeper thoughts)

It's been a busy week and tomorrow is a "no school" day, so I figure I better catch up in my diary (wouldn't want to leave an important piece of my life out!). This week we've had a lot of Martin Luther King Jr. activities going on at our school, which I actually think is pretty cool. I even wrote an essay on him, and although I know he wasn't perfect or anything, I think he was a pretty amazing guy and I really do admire all he did for human rights and everything.

So I'm sitting here wondering, will my life ever have any important significance like that? I know I'll never do anything as important as Reverend King, but sometimes I hope that my life will amount to <u>something</u> beyond just education and career and getting married and having kids (not that I see <u>that</u> happening any time soon!). But, it's like, I look at my parents' lives and I think—there's got to be more to life than that. Oh yeah, I'll admit the idea of meeting Mr. Wonderful (and I must confess I still dream about Josh Miller occasionally) and getting married can sound pretty good sometimes. But still, it just seems there should be more to life than that. Only, I'm not sure what. And I'm not even sure what's making me so philosophical today—maybe it's just all this Martin Luther King Jr. stuff. And I suppose it's good for everyone to think a little more deeply from time to time.

Speaking of deep thinkers, I talked to Beanie this week. I was feeling kind of bad and I just decided to call her up and see how she was doing and everything. She sounded so down and depressed, and I kept thinking is this all my fault? But then how can I take responsibility for someone else's life when I don't even quite know what to do with my own?

But anyway, I told her I was sorry that I hadn't spent time with her lately, but that my life was just taking another direction. Beanie was actually pretty under-standing, even if she was slightly sarcastic about it. She said she knew that "my little stint with popularity had become all consuming for me, but that it probably wouldn't last forever." I figured I probably deserved that, and didn't even get defensive. I just told her that I hoped everything was going okay for her and that I'd see her around. To which she laughed and said, "Around where?" I can't remember what I said after that, but then I just hung up. Somehow that conversation didn't go exactly where I thought it would, but then I don't even know where that was. But perhaps I just needed to have some closure, as my mom likes to say.

The truth is I think I may have closed the door on my friendship with Beanie forever. And I have to admit that makes me feel pretty crappy. Because the fact is, I never feel as relaxed or have as much fun with Jenny and her friends as I used to have with good old Beanie. I always feel like I have to be really careful and act just right when I'm with Jenny (like she wouldn't like me if I acted like the geek that I sometimes suspect I really am). Okay, enough true confessions, this diary is really getting me down today. Maybe I should only write about what's going on in my life—not about how everything makes me feel.

February 2, Friday (official first date)

I can't believe it's been so long since I've written in here. But life's been so busy lately—a good thing, I think. And now, even though it's really late tonight, I want to try to catch up a little. Let's see, Jenny and Josh are still together, although as much as she complains about him, I wonder why she doesn't just let someone else (like me) give him a chance. Fat chance!

So, anyway, Nathan started talking to me again, and I actually do like him. Plus he's a pretty good distraction from Josh. Although Josh and I have become good friends now, and frankly I don't see why Jenny is so down on him all the time. But I try not to think about that too much. Anyway, Nathan invited me to go to the aftergame dance with him tonight, and Mom said it was okay! Fortunately, Dad wasn't around when I asked (he seems to be gone more and more—handy for me right now, but I think it's bugging my mom, and Benjamin is acting like a total brat boy!) but so much for the home front.

So anyway, Nathan and I went to the dance together. And I guess you'd say it was my first official date (I mean I've done stuff with guys and girls in youth group) but this was the first time it was just me and a boy alone in a car and going someplace together. And it was pretty fun.

Nathan has medium brown hair and kind of hazel eyes. He's tall (six-foot-three to be exact) and he has this really great laugh (kind of deep, but sweet). It was nice being around other kids at the dance; it kind of took the pressure off of having to be such a great conversationalist. And we mixed it up a little too (dancing with other kids) and I even got to dance <u>twice</u> with Josh. Dreamy. But that's all I'll say about that!

Nathan is really nice, and unlike some of the kids, he didn't sneak any alcohol into the dance. A relief when it came time for him to take me home. And despite my dad's assumption that high school boys only want one thing, Nathan acted like a perfect gentleman. Although he did kiss me good-night in the car (a relief that he didn't try it at the front door, just in case my dad was watching). But anyway, let me say this (it wasn't my first kiss or anything—that happened back at a spin-the-bottle game at middle school church camp): this wasn't a really great kiss. It was more like a quick peck, and I certainly didn't feel any fireworks or anything earthshaking. So, I just said good-night and got out of the car and quickly went into the house (I was kind of glad Nathan didn't walk me to the door). And thankfully my parents weren't lurking around and I just zipped straight upstairs to my room.

But now I'm wondering, was it <u>my</u> fault that it wasn't a good kiss? Was it because I kept thinking about Josh the whole time? Anyway, I guess the right thing would be to just nicely break things off with Nathan. Suddenly, I don't feel like I want to go out on any more dates right now.

Well, okay, maybe if it was with Josh, I might consider it. (Okay, I'd totally leap at the chance!) But he and Jenny seemed happier than ever with each other tonight, so I'm sure I'll never get a chance with him. I guess I should just enjoy being his friend—not every girl gets that opportunity!

FIVE

February 6, Tuesday (users and losers)

It's just four days until the Valentine's Day dance and now Jenny and I, and several other (totally hopeless nerd-type) honor society kids will have to work like crazy to get all the decorations made in time. Surprisingly enough (since I've been acting sort of chilly) Nathan is still talking to me, and has even called me at home a couple of times, and I keep telling myself that we're nothing more than friends, although I strongly suspect he thinks there's something more going on (or that there will be before long). I guess maybe I should've broken it off sooner, but I just never had the right opportunity, and I have to admit this whole guy-girl thing is still sort of new to me.

Fortunately, Nathan has so much basketball practice during the week (and a game tonight which I'm <u>not</u> going to—thanks to my grades dropping sort of unexpectedly this last semester and now my dad's all over me like a bad case of zits). There really hasn't been all that much spare time for me to spend with Nathan (not that I've really wanted to). So I guess I'm just sort of going along with everything right now (like everyone assuming that we're a couple).

But let me be totally honest about this—you see, I really do want to go to the Valentine's Dance (and I don't want to go alone and look like a geek), and Nathan asked me to go with him. And, I ask you, what other prospects did I have? I mean, just a couple of months ago, I would've done back flips at the chance to go <u>anywhere</u> with someone as popular as Nathan Parker. But now, it's like I'm just using <u>him</u>. Is that lame or what? But I'm afraid it's the pitiful truth. And although part of me feels totally guilty for using him like this, on the other hand, I'm wondering why can't you just be friends with a boy and go to a dance together? I mean, is that so bad?

I guess the part that makes it bad is that I'm actually hoping I'll get to dance with Josh while I'm there. And I'm also hoping that Josh's eyes will pop out and roll across the cafeteria floor when he sees me in my powder-pink satin dress that Mom let me get last weekend (with Grandma chipping in as well, she said it was my Valentine's present). Jenny went with us and helped me to pick it out, and she said that color looked absolutely fantastic with my pale blond hair (Jenny's dress is a similar style, only hers is burgundy which doesn't look half bad with her dark hair).

Anyway, I know I've got all kinds of horribly wrong

motives going on here, and the whole guilt thing is starting to get to me a little, but I just can't seem to help myself. Am I hopeless, or what? Sometimes I look at myself in the mirror and I wonder what someone like Beanie Jacobs would say to me right now (that is if she was even talking to me, which she isn't by the way). She'd probably accuse me of having sold my soul to the devil. To tell the truth, sometimes it almost feels like I did. But I didn't. At least I'm pretty sure I didn't. I don't remember shaking hands or signing anything binding....

February 10, Saturday (the big dance)

Well, talk about your let-downs. I guess I should've known the night was doomed when my dad went ballistic the instant he saw me in my pink dress (did I mention it was strapless?). Well, my poor dad (too bad we didn't have any tranquilizers on hand) just totally flipped out. "You're not leaving the house in that—that slip!" I think you'd call it blustering. Anyway, he went on and on, his face growing redder by the moment and the veins visibly popping out in his neck (I was actually worried he was going to have an honest-to-goodness stroke and we'd have to take him to the hospital and I'd miss the dance altogether, which might not have been such a bad thing after all). Anyway, my mom couldn't even calm him down. And of course, it didn't help any when Benjamin threw in his two cents, saying that I looked like Marilyn Monroe (I mean, how does <u>he</u> even know who Marilyn Monroe is, or was?). And then just as my parents began getting into what sounded like a horrible fight over the whole thing, I saw Nathan's car pull up outside.

So I just waved good-bye and streaked out the door like a powder-pink flash. I explained to Nathan that my parents were in there going totally nuts and the safest thing was just to get away as quickly as possible. Of course, he thought I was joking and laughed.

Anyway, we went to the dance (and the decorations looked pretty good even if I do say so myself). We sat with Jenny and Josh and a bunch of other kids, and just when things started getting fun, Jenny said she felt sick and asked Josh to take her home. And—boom—they were gone. Suddenly, everything at the dance seemed to go totally flat for me, and I didn't even care if I was there or not. But I tried to paste on a happy face for Nathan's sake (I mean he'd brought me a wrist corsage and everything). It's bad enough that I was using him, but at least I wanted him to think <u>he</u> was having a good time.

I can't really remember too much about the evening after that—at least not until Nathan spilled a whole cup of red Hawaiian punch down the front of my dress. Well, needless to say, I wasn't too happy about that (imagine pale pink streaked in bright red—it's not a pretty picture). But just the same, I tried really hard not to make <u>too</u> big of a deal out of it. Then finally, I think Nathan suspected I wasn't having all that much fun, and he suggested we might like to leave early, which I gladly agreed to.

Then as we were driving home, he asked if I wanted

to join Josh and Jenny. Surprised, I said, "But I thought Josh took Jenny home because she was sick." Nathan just laughed, and then explained how Josh and Jenny had gone to a hotel where Josh had reserved a room for the night. Apparently several other couples were doing the same thing. Well, I'd heard about kids doing stuff like this on prom night, but for some reason this kind of took me by surprise. So, feeling fed up with Nathan and everything else, I told him that I preferred to go home. (Home, to my flipped-out family was what I was thinking.) So, without saying much more, Nathan took me home. And I have a feeling we won't be going out again. Which, I must admit, is something of a relief.

Fortunately, when I got home, my parents weren't around. I wasn't real eager for Mom to see that awful stain on my dress (which I doubt will ever come out). But somehow, I thought she might like to hear about how everything had gone. It's not like I'd gotten home all that late or anything. Then I wondered if perhaps my parents had made up after their big fight and gone out to a movie or something. (They say that Benjamin is old enough to be left home alone now that he's twelve, which I happen to think is totally ridiculous—that kid is more dangerous now than when he was seven!)

So I peeked in the garage to see that Dad's car was gone. But then on my way to my room, I walked past my parents' door and heard my mom in there—<u>crying</u>. I wanted to ask her what was wrong, but somehow I just couldn't make myself do it. Maybe it was the awful stain on my dress—or maybe it was something more—like some sort of childish denial where you want to believe that your parents are special, like they have some secret marriage formula that guarantees that they'll never have problems, ever. But, of course, I know that's not really true. I just don't want to know anything more about it tonight. I mean, it's already been a pretty rotten evening. Why make things worse?

February 11, Sunday (a revelation)

My dad never did come home last night, and this morning we didn't even go to church (which didn't bother me in the least). My mom slept in and when she got up she had these dark circles under her eyes. And I felt really sorry for her. I think Ben did too, because he actually managed to keep his big mouth shut for the most part. In the afternoon, when I just couldn't stand the silence anymore, I sat down next to her in the living room (where she had been sitting on the sofa for the last hour or so, still wearing her robe) and I asked her what was going on. She just waved her hand and said, "Oh, it's really nothing." So, without beating around the bush, I asked her why Dad never came home last night. And she said they'd had a little spat, but not to worry, everything would be okay, and that she was probably just having a bad case of PMS. Nice try, Mom.

But then suddenly it hits me and I totally realize what is going on here. They are fighting over me! And now I feel absolutely miserable. Of course, it all makes sense, lately I've become so self-centered with my new friends and popularity, and I started dating (against my dad's wishes) and then I wear this expensive and what my dad considers "indecent" dress. I can see now I've pitted my parents against each other and I feel really bad about it. So, I throw my arms around my mom and tell her how sorry I am, and how everything is going to get better—just wait and see!

I know this unexpected display surprised my mom a little, but she did seem comforted by my concern. Anyway, I decided not to say too much about it just yet. My plan is to wait and talk to my dad directly. Unfortunately, he hasn't come home at all today, which does have me a little worried, but I know if I can only talk to him for a little while, and tell him I'm sorry, and how I want to stick to his no-dating rule and everything— then I'm absolutely certain that everything will get back to normal around here. And the truth is, I don't really care whether I ever date again—well, at least not for a long, long time.

Okay, I guess, that is, unless Josh and Jenny should somehow break up, which isn't at all likely considering what they were up to last night (something I'd really rather not think about). No, I seriously doubt that they'll be breaking up anytime real soon. And all of a sudden, I wonder what Beanie Baby is up to these days. And I'm even thinking about giving her a call!

February 13, Tuesday (a very bad day)

Right now I'm so furious, so totally angry (#@!!#!) I can
hardly hold this pen straight in my hand to write all this
down! First off, my dad never did come home. Mom said
he'd called her to tell her he was okay, but that he just
wanted to take a little time away to figure things out.
And actually, Mom seemed slightly better about everything too. But I really wanted to talk to Dad and explain
how I wasn't going to date anymore, and how sorry I was
that I came between my parents like that. So after
school, I asked Jenny if she could drop me by his office
today (he works in this big ad agency downtown). Anyway,
she didn't mind at all.

Now, of course, that meant I had to sit there and listen to her go on and on about how wonderful it had been
with Josh the other night (when they went to that stupid
hotel!). I mean, I just wanted to scream at her to shut up
about the whole moronic thing! Is she so clueless as to not
understand that I have absolutely no desire to hear
about it—and I don't care if it was her first time to do
it. I just tried to block out all of her words and to stare
out the window, and somehow I managed to keep my
mouth closed and to control myself from telling her that I
thought she was being incredibly stupid, and that she'd
be lucky not to get some horrible STD, or worse yet, even
pregnant! Because, I reminded myself, she was after all
giving me a free ride.

And so there I sat as we drove through the business

section, politely ignoring her constant babbling, letting her words float right over me, and focusing my thoughts on how sad and hopeless my mom had looked on Sunday when my dad didn't come home. I told myself I was on a mission of mercy to save my family, and if that meant subjecting myself to Jenny's blathering on about Josh (the boy I'd thought I loved) then it was just the price I had to pay for having been such a complete idiot in the first place.

And finally, we were there, and I thanked her and told her that I'd catch a ride home with my dad. Even though I really wished I could talk to someone, I haven't told Jenny anything about my parents' recent marital problems. Somehow I just don't think she'd care all that much, especially now that she's so wrapped up in her new and exciting sex life with Josh Miller!

So, there I was riding the elevator up to my dad's office, rehearsing my little repentance speech, and imagining my dad's relief to see me and hear how sorry I am about all this. But, of course, he's in a meeting. I guess I should've known, that man's always in meetings.

"You can wait in his office, dear," says old Mrs. Greenly, smiling just as pleasantly as ever. (My mom says that she takes happy pills, because no matter how chaotic things get at the office, she somehow keeps every gray hair perfectly in place, and nothing at all ever seems to disturb her.) So anyway, I go into my dad's office (and it occurs to me that I haven't been here for at least a couple of years) and I sit in his black leather chair and lean back, pretending like I'm some big high-level executive, running a multimillion dollar fashion corporation. Who knows, it could happen. Everything in my dad's office is either black or gray or chrome—very uptown and classy. Image is everything, they say in the advertising world, and I suppose in some ways I've fallen victim to that same sort of thinking. But after waiting for about twenty minutes, my stomach begins to rumble (I still have difficulty eating in front of Jenny and her friends at school) and suddenly I'm wondering if Dad still keeps a supply of Snickers bars hidden somewhere in his desk, and I eagerly begin to search through his orderly desk drawers. And that's when I find it.

At first when I see the long narrow velvet box (obviously from a fairly nice jewelry store), I think it must be something for Mom, probably an "I'm sorry" sort of Valentine's Day gift (which is tomorrow by the way). But then I see a white envelope just beneath it—and the name on the envelope doesn't say "Karen" (my mom's name) but the name "Belinda" is written neatly on it (in Dad's precise handwriting)! What in the world is this about, I'm wondering, afraid to even consider the ramifications of something like this. So, I figure as long as I've gone this far, I decide I might as well open the box—and inside I see this delicate gold bracelet with what I suspect to be some real diamonds (even if they are somewhat small). I snap the box closed, my heart pounding in my throat. I can't believe it! Does _my_ dad have a girl-friend? Then I glance quickly over to the still open door, certain that I'll be caught snooping.

But no one is watching, so I pick up the smooth white envelope to discover that the back isn't properly sealed (stupid move, Dad). And even though I know it's wrong to look, I also need to know the truth. Of course, it's this totally sappy, lovesick Valentine poem, obviously a feeble attempt for Dad to proclaim his "love and devotion" to this Belinda person—<u>not my mother</u>! With totally shaking hands, I stuff the stupid card back into the envelope and shove both these detestable objects back into his lower desk drawer. I don't even do it very carefully. Why should I care if he thinks someone saw it—I mean, he's the one who's got a problem here!!!

Now, all I can think of is that I've got to get out of here—and fast! I do <u>not</u> want to see my dad! And when Mrs. Greenly asks why I'm leaving so soon, I can't even answer, and so she just nods and says, "Well then, good-bye, dear, have a nice day," just as if my entire world wasn't crashing down all around me!

And so I ride the elevator back down, certain that I'm going to puke all over the gray carpeting, but somehow I make it back outside where a cold wind is starting to blow and cuts right through my thin jacket like a steel blade that's slicing right into my heart. And suddenly I feel the tears nearly freezing right on my cheeks. But I keep walking away from the office building, until I finally reach the bus stop a couple blocks down the street. And then I sit down on the cold metal bench and cry.

I've never ridden the bus from downtown like that,

but somehow I managed to do it all just right, and after I got off I only had to walk about eight more blocks to get home. (It's actually a pretty decent transit system we have in this town.) Then I go straight to my room and cry some more. And that's where I've been all night. I never even went down for dinner. I told Mom I was having really bad cramps (the best I could come up with). I can't stand to look into her eyes right now. I mean, how can I possibly keep a secret like this away from her? Yet how can I possibly tell her? I am so utterly miserable.

I can't believe it. Here, I was ready to take all the blame for my parents' problems. I thought their little spat was totally my fault. Now I <u>wish</u> that it were. Oh, if only it were.

SIX

Wednesday, February 14 (happy Valentine's Day)

It feels like my entire life is falling apart—on absolutely every level. For starters there's this awful thing with my parents. (I've managed to avoid my mom since yesterday, but how long can that possibly last?) And now she's down in the kitchen fixing this big special dinner, thinking that my dad's going to come home and everything's going to be just fine. Oh brother! And yet, what if he DOES come home? What will I say to him? How can I pretend that I don't know something is going on with him and that Belinda person?

Well, okay, and if that's not enough, I got into this big, ugly fight with Jenny at lunchtime today. Okay, now you're probably thinking, why should I even care—I mean, only yesterday I wanted to just totally tell her off. But the funny thing is, <u>she's the one</u> who started the fight in the first place. Which I suppose was lucky for me, because Heather actually sided with me and told Jenny she was acting like a total moron. But just the same it really hurt to hear Jenny lashing into me like that, especially in front of <u>everyone</u>—and all because of some stupid anonymous Valentine that some idiot (probably one of the youth group geeks) stuck in my locker. I only showed it to my friends for a few laughs (which I could've really used today!). But for some reason Jenny just exploded and said that I was showing off. (<u>Me</u> showing off! Ha! As if I don't know how barely in their little clique I even am!) But instead of backing down and just taking it, like I would've done a few weeks ago, I just gave it right back to her. Man, you should've heard us yelling at each other.

I felt kind of bad about the whole thing later, that is until Heather told me that the reason Jenny was in such a foul mood was because Josh hadn't gotten her a Valentine. Oh brother, give me a break! But then I started thinking about the whole thing differently during my creative writing class. (Which I happen to really like, and I think it has a lot to do with writing in this diary, and Miss Tyler says I'm a very good writer.) I was thinking about how that must make Jenny feel. I mean, less than a week after she does <u>it</u> for the very first time, and then Josh can't even give her a stupid Valentine.

Well, let me tell you, Josh had already dropped down quite a few notches on my list anyway, but this really makes me see him in a brand new light. And I think if I get the chance I might even tell him face to face what a complete jerk I think he is. I can't believe how bold I've gotten all of the sudden—it's like I don't even care what

these kids think of me anymore. I could just take their
popularity or leave it. And quite frankly, I'm thinking I
might be better off without them anyway. (Although I'm
not completely sure about that.) And it's quite possible
that this whole thing with my parents is affecting my
thinking right now.

But anyway, I was actually feeling sort of sorry for
Jenny, so I stopped by the student store and got her a
cheesy little Valentine card and a cherry Charms
sucker, and stuck them both in the slots of her locker.
She'll probably just throw them away. Not that I really
care (okay, so maybe I do). All I can say is at least I
tried. Now, I just hope I don't have to face my dad
tonight (not that he's likely to come home, I mean after
giving his little girlfriend that bracelet, they've probably
cozier than ever right now—poor Mom!). But if he did happen to show his face on the home front, I'm afraid after
all this venting that went on at school today, I might just
speak my mind to him about this stupid Belinda person—
and then I cannot even imagine what my mom would
think about that. Or is it possible that she already knows?

So, happy Valentine's day to you too!

Thursday, February 15 (some consolation)

My dad never showed up for Mom's special Valentine's dinner last night. He called and they talked for a few minutes, but her voice was so quiet I couldn't make out any
of the words. Then she and Ben and I ate her home-
made lasagna by candlelight. I got to wondering if this

was the way it would be from now on—just the three of us. It was weird. Ben keeps asking where Dad is, and Mom just keeps making up all these excuses for him, saying that he's really busy with work and stuff (which sounds pretty believable considering how much of the time he'd been gone lately, and now I'm wondering if it was all really work-related or not).

But the point is, I am so unbelievably furious at him. What a total hypocrite! I mean, I'm thinking about all those stupid sermons he gave to me about how "the only thing high school boys are interested in is one thing!" Man, he must've been talking from his own personal experience (thinking he's like some stupid high school kid having this secret little romance! UGH!). But, wait a minute, I thought stuff like this wasn't supposed to happen to good, church-going Christians. What are his Bible study buddies going to say about <u>this</u>, I wonder. Oh, I'm just so incredibly mad, I can hardly put my thoughts into words. The whole thing just makes me want to scream! And how long does he plan to stay away without telling us what's really going on? Isn't that a crappy thing to do?

I honestly don't think I'll ever be able to forgive him for all this—not to mention he has totally lost my respect forever!

I've got to change the subject or I am just going to totally explode and go splatting across my room in tiny little pieces. Take a deep breath, Caitlin, just relax now, calm down.

Okay, well at least something good happened to me

today. When I got to school this morning, Jenny was waiting by my locker. And to my surprise, she just threw her arms around me and apologized. Well, I was so shocked I almost fell over. And stupidly enough, I got a little teary-eyed. But then I've been under a lot of strain lately. She said, "I'm sorry I was such a total idiot yesterday. I was just all worried about what was going on between me and Josh." I nodded and said it was okay and that I was sorry too. Then without thinking I blurted out what was going on with my parents and how it had me all stressed out. At first I thought it was a big mistake, but Jenny was actually quite understanding and sympathetic.

She pointed out that my dad was probably just going through a midlife crisis and that he'd get over it eventually, and that everything would be back to normal before I knew it. With honest skepticism, I asked her how she could be so sure, and she said that the exact same thing had happened to her parents about a year ago, and that everything worked itself out, and that, by the way, was why her mom got that slick new BMW for Christmas and, of course, why Jenny now has her own car.

"Just think," she said with her usual confidence. "By summer you might be driving your mom's car." Well, I had to laugh at that one. But it's something to hope for. Anyway, I'll try to take Jenny's advice and not get too worried about the whole thing. Although I have to admit I've even been feeling sorry for Benjamin lately (he's been acting kind of strange and I think the whole thing is pretty hard on him too), and as a result I was actually nice to him this morning and let him have the last bowl of Cheerios.

Friday, February 16 (something's happening here)

A really weird thing happened tonight, actually a couple of weird things. But one in particular that I don't even know what to make of. Anyway, after the game a bunch of us went over to Jenny's house. It wasn't a party or anything, although her parents weren't there, and she did get into their bar which they assume always remains locked up when they're away, but they don't realize she has her own key! But no one was really getting drunk or anything wild like I've seen at some of the other parties. Instead we were just sitting around talking and stuff, acting fairly adult.

So, the first weird thing that happened tonight, was that I actually had a drink. Okay, let me tell you why. I figure that if my dad can preach at me about how to live my life so perfectly and everything, and then he goes off and does—well whatever it is he's doing—then why in the world should I listen to, or even respect, a single word he has to say? I mean, it's not like I plan on going totally crazy and becoming some wild child—I know that would be incredibly stupid. I figure, what's one drink going to hurt? Besides it didn't even taste good!

But here's the second weird thing, and this one's

really got me wondering. When it was time to clear out (because Jenny's parents were supposed to be getting back from their movie any minute), Josh offered to drop me off on his way home. Well, now that Josh and Jenny seem to be doing okay (and I try and repress any feelings—good or bad—that I have for him), I thought, sure, why not? Jenny didn't seem to mind a bit, she mostly just wanted to get everyone out of there before her parents got back. So Josh drives me home. And we talk as he drives and suddenly I'm thinking, man, this is the guy I always thought he was. I mean, he sounds all smart and thoughtful, and I almost forget that he is actually going with Jenny.

Then at my house, we're sitting out in front talking about (I kid you not) world peace. And suddenly he leans over towards me, and I swear he's about to kiss me! Well, I am so shocked that I pull away, jump right out of the Jeep, and dash into the house (real mature, I know). But Jenny is practically my best friend now, and we already had one big blowout that left me feeling pretty miserable, and now she's being all understanding about my parents and everything. So, how could I do that to her?

But, let me be truthful, as soon as I was in the house, I wanted to turn around and get back in the car, and take it right from where we left off. Of course, his little Jeep was completely out of sight by then. For which, I'm sure, I should be very thankful. But what in the world was _that_ all about? And how do I act the next time I see him? And, of course, I can never tell Jenny. Now I'm starting to wonder if I didn't just imagine the whole thing in the first place. I know I have (what Beanie used to call) a hyperactive imagination. And then how embarrassing would that be? I mean, for me just to leap out of his car without any explanation, and without even thanking him for bringing me home, and all he was going to do was open the door for me or something.

But I don't really think it was my imagination. He had a certain look on his face (at least I think he did). And now I'll probably dream about him and that old crush thing will start up all over again. Oh brother!

Saturday, February 17 (clearing the air)

My dad came home today. Apparently it wasn't his first time to drop in. Mom told me that he'd already been by while we were away at school to pick up some clothes and things. According to Mom, he's been staying with his friend, Brad Schielbert, at work. Although I wonder if he might actually be staying with Belinda (whoever she is— and for some reason, I keep imagining her as this flashy little brunette who wears way too much makeup).

My dad wanted to sit down and talk to Ben and me about everything while he was here. Mom had already left the house by then; I think they had worked the whole thing out ahead of time. Anyway, I sat like a stone on the sofa while Dad explained that he had reached a difficult place in his life where he needed some time and space to figure some things out. (Yeah sure, I thought, you just need some time and space to be with your beloved Belinda, you big, old hypocrite! But I kept silent.)

Ben asked some questions, and I could tell by his voice he was almost crying. Poor Ben, I think this is even going to be harder on him than it is on me—I mean, at least I only have a year and a half at home before I go off to college. But Ben's only twelve. I'm sure my dad could tell by my sour expression that I wasn't taking this whole thing real well, and when he was all finished talking, he turned to me and said, "Are you going to be okay with all this?"

Then I just looked him straight in the eye and said, "Do you really care?"

Of course, he said he did. And then I told him if he wanted to hear what I thought, he'd better hear it in private. I think this surprised him a little. Then he asked if we both wanted to go have lunch with him. I told him no thanks, but maybe he should take Ben. And while Ben went upstairs to get his coat, in a very controlled voice, I told Dad that I knew all about Belinda. And furthermore, I told him that I thought he was a liar and a hypocrite and that I no longer respected anything he had to say about church or Christianity or anything for that matter. Then I turned and ran up the stairs before he could say anything. And what, I ask, could he possibly say to that?

But at least I got it off my chest. Then I threw myself across my bed and cried really hard for a long, long time.

So, why did God let this happen to us? I mean, here

my family's been going along just fine—all things considered, we were doing pretty well—going to church sometimes and sticking together all these years without any great, big problems. So, why this? Why now? I just don't get it. And frankly, it just doesn't seem fair.

SEVEN

Sunday, February 18 (picking up the pieces)

For the second Sunday in a row, we
didn't go to church today. Not that I really care. I think
if God turned his back on us, then we might as well turn
our backs on him too. Do you think I could be struck by
lightning for writing something like that? Oh well, it might
be for the best since I just seem to be making a perfect
mess of everything anyway.

Okay, here's what happened. Last night I was feeling
pretty grumpy. For one thing, there was nothing to do, and
Jenny hadn't called all day, and I didn't call her
because I'm still feeling guilty about what Josh tried (at
least I think he tried) the other night. So anyway, I was
just hanging around being your basic grump and naturally
ended up having a fight with my little brother, who was
acting like a total moron and had just made this huge
mess in the bathroom that we have to share and I
thought <u>he</u> should clean up (what I wouldn't do for my
<u>own</u> bathroom like Jenny has).

Anyway, Mom actually had to come in and break us apart (Ben's almost as tall as me now and was getting a little carried away). It was pretty embarrassing to need Mom's help in fending off my little brother (and I seriously doubt that I'll be engaging in any more tangles like that with him real soon). I did feel slightly bad 'cause I know Ben's pretty upset about all this crud with Dad.

Well as a result, Mom took me into her room to talk, saying all this stuff about how she really needed my help right now, and how I had to take more responsibility and everything. I told her I would try. Then she asked how our talk had gone with my dad today. Well, I couldn't look her in the eye and answer honestly, so I just said "it went okay." Then she was acting all understanding and compassionate towards Dad, saying that we just needed to be patient and allow him this time to figure things out.

Well, that was just too much! So I said, "What are you talking about? Are you going to just sit around here waiting while he figures things out with Belinda?" And it was like I had slapped here across the face. The expression of pain that came in her eyes was more than I could stand to look at, as she asked in a shaky voice, "Who's Belinda?"

And then, of course, I just burst into tears and told her the whole sorry story. I mean, what am I supposed to do—she's my mom for crud's sake!

Now talk about a really bad scene. My mom just totally fell to pieces at this bit of news. And I didn't know what to do. Should I call 911? Grandma? No, I decided, this is a job for Aunt Stephie—she's the expert in the area of broken hearts. Thank goodness Steph was home, and she bundled up baby Oliver and rushed right over. As penance I baby-sat Oliver all night while Stephie took Mom out to talk. I don't know where they went, but they didn't get home until late. And Stephie ended up spending the night and most of the day today. But I must admit, it's good to have her here and I don't even mind helping with Oliver (who is just starting to walk and is getting into everything and has just about totally demolished my entire room!).

But here's something unexpected—Aunt Stephie actually wanted us to go to church this morning! At first we thought she was kidding—I mean, this is Stephie the "wild child" as my dad used to call her. And now she's trying to get <u>us</u> to go to church. Mom explained she didn't really want to go to church without Dad and have to tell everyone what was going on. But then, wonder of wonders, Stephie says, "No, I meant you should come to <u>my</u> church."

And so, it turns out, that Aunt Stephie has begun going to church of all things! I guess someone at the bank, where she works as a teller, invited her around Christmastime to this new church that's meeting in one of the grade schools. And Stephie dressed Oliver up in a little suit and just went. And she said the people there are all very real and that it was nothing like any church she's ever been to before (apparently they have a band that plays with drums and electric guitars and everything), and she's been going pretty regularly ever since. Well, you just never know! But just the same, we weren't in the mood for church this morning, and Mom told her maybe next week, and Stephie said she's holding us to it.

February 21, Wednesday (confusing confessions)

So far this week's been fairly uneventful. Stephie has been over at our house a lot, and she and Mom seem closer than ever before. This takes a big load off of me, and even Ben seems to be adjusting a little better now. He announced today that he's going to try out for the sixth-grade baseball team, and seems pretty happy about it.

My dad called to talk to me yesterday evening. I almost hung up, then decided to hear what he had to say. Naturally, he asked me how I knew about Belinda, and I told him about the bracelet. Then he had the audacity to say that he has not been unfaithful to my mom. So I said, "What do you mean?"

And then there was this long silence and finally he said, "I haven't had an actual affair with Belinda yet." It was the yet that caught me.

"Then you're considering it?" I said accusingly. Another long silence.

"I want to be honest with you, Catie," he said. "Yes, I've been thinking about it." I didn't know whether to believe him or not—whether to yell at him or simply hang up? But somehow I managed to stay on the line.

"Well, isn't there a verse in the Bible that says if you think about something, it's just like actually doing it?" (I could hardly believe I came up with that line, but all those years of going to church shouldn't be for nothing!) He coughed slightly, kind of like he choked on something. Then I continued. "You know you used to give me all those stupid talks about boys and dating and all that crud—and the whole time you were off <u>thinking</u> about cheating on your wife!"

Now I was just waiting for him to hang up on <u>me</u>. But surprisingly, he didn't. Instead he said, "I guess I deserve that." His voice sounded so sad that I almost felt sorry for my harsh words. Almost.

Then I said, "So, Dad, if you haven't cheated yet, what's stopping you?" I couldn't believe we were even having this conversation. I mean, when had everything changed so drastically; when had the earth shifted on its axis?

"I don't know," he answered quietly. "I'm just trying to figure it all out—I don't want to destroy everything—"

"Do you still love Mom?" I demanded.

"I think so, but I don't know..."

Then I thought again of all that church stuff and his Bible study friends. "Do you still believe in God and all that crud you used to go on and on about—or are you trying to figure all that out too?"

His voice grew stern now. "It's not crud, Caitlin. Just because I'm having some trials right now doesn't mean that anything I've taught you was wrong—"

I cut him off again. "But it means that it doesn't work. Does it Dad? I mean, it obviously hasn't worked for you. How can I expect that it will work for me?" By then my voice was getting all ragged with tears (I can only take so much of this confrontational stuff until I fall apart) and so I had to hang up on him.

I just couldn't bear for him to know that he had actually made me cry. I don't want him to think I care enough to cry.

And now I'm sitting here wondering about all that stuff. God, the Bible, church—all of it. What good has it done my parents? What good has it done me? And, besides, how can I base my entire belief system on my parents' beliefs (which seems to be failing them miserably, by the way). I've considered discussing all this with Aunt Stephie, but she seems to have her hands full with my mom right now. And besides, everyone knows that Stephie is kind of flaky. I mean, she can be madly in love with a guy one day, and then hate him the next. Who's to say she won't be the same way about this new church of hers? No, it may be best to ponder these things in private. Figure it out for myself.

February 23. Thursday (a surprising invitation)

Something very strange happened today. I went to the library during my study period. I had decided to find a book about religion and do some research for myself. I know that may sound slightly obsessive, but all these questions about God and religion are so confusing, so I thought I just might find some answers in this book.

Anyway, I had just settled down to do some serious

reading when Josh Miller comes in and sits down right beside me. Well, naturally, I just act all nonchalant and cool (the way I'd been acting toward him all week, but usually Jenny is around to sort of buffer things). And so he asks me what I'm reading. Sort of embarrassed, I show him the front of the book, and explain I'm trying to under-stand things better. I figure he'll probably make fun of me, but oddly enough he doesn't. Instead, he says that he understands how I feel, and that he's been trying to get his life right with God lately too.

I'm just about dumbfounded at that. I mean, give me a break—how can it be that Josh Miller, the most popular boy in school, is trying to get his life right with God? Then he tells me about the youth pastor in his church and how he's been talking to him a lot lately.

"You go to church?" I ask incredulously. To which he laughs and says, "Sure, why not?" Then he tells me that he knows he's got some things wrong in his life and he really wants to get things straightened out before he goes off to the state college next year. Then he gets real serious and tells me about his older brother who went to college and got totally messed up with alcohol and drugs and ended up dropping out and now his par-ents don't even know where he is or if he's even doing okay.

"It's weird because Caleb was always the smart one, getting straight A's and stuff like that," he tells me sadly. "But look what happened to him. I don't want to end up like that. I don't think my parents could take it."

I was totally amazed—and I thought I had this guy all figured out. So, I closed my book and looked at him. "Well, it sounds like you don't need to worry about that, Josh. It looks like you've got your head on pretty straight." He smiled, then said he wasn't so sure.

But then here's the real shocker—he asked if I wanted to come on a ski retreat that his youth group was having the weekend after next. I shrugged and said, "Sure, why not?" thinking he probably wasn't serious. Then he promised to bring me all the sign-up information tomorrow.

"Is Jenny coming too?" I asked, figuring this was a no-brainer.

"No," he said. "She thinks church is stupid. I can never get her to come to anything. It's one of the many things we don't agree on." I nodded dumbly, but I really wanted to ask, if you don't agree on so many things, then why do you two stay together? But then Jenny is a good (almost best) friend. How could I say something like that to her boyfriend?

But now I'm wondering, should I tell Jenny about this upcoming ski trip? Did Josh even ask her to come? And what if she gets jealous or mad? Maybe I better just keep my mouth shut. I mean, it's not like Josh is asking me to go out with him or anything. He just saw me sitting there reading about religion and he wanted to help out. All he did was tell me about his youth group and a retreat I might enjoy. What's wrong with that?

But I'll be honest and tell you exactly what's wrong with that—my motives. It's like the Valentine's Dance all over again. I'm not going on that retreat to learn more about God (well, not completely anyway). I'm going because I want Josh to notice me. I want him to forget all about Jenny and to fall head over heels in love with me. And for that reason I think I'm totally despicable.

February 25, Sunday (Stephie's church)

We went to church with Aunt Stephie today. I wanted to bail, but Stephie wouldn't hear of it, and I could tell Mom wanted us to all go together. Especially after what happened last night.

You see, my dad came over to the house to talk with all of us. My mom just totally blew up at him. I suppose it was my fault because I let the whole Belinda thing out of the bag and she, like me, just naturally assumed that my dad was sleeping with the little tramp. In fact, even now, I'm not totally sure he's not. However, he swore up and down that he was <u>not</u> having an actual affair with her. (Poor Benjamin had to hear the whole thing too, but then he's not a baby anymore—welcome to the adult world, baby brother!) But Dad did admit that he had been tempted to, and was trying to figure everything all out (I'm getting so sick and tired of hearing <u>that</u>!).

He kept saying he didn't want to lose everything—his family, his church, his home. But finally, I just couldn't take it anymore, and I blurted out, "You mean you just want to <u>have it all</u>, Dad? You think you can be a good husband, a good dad, and then just keep your little girlfriend on the side?" Well, as you can imagine, he didn't say anything to that. Then I stormed off to my room. It's the only way to hide the tears (and they were about to pour). Then I heard Mom take it from there, and pretty soon even Benjamin was yelling too.

I almost felt sorry for Dad. But only for a few seconds. And suddenly, I wondered, who is this Belinda person anyway? What sort of woman would want to come between my parents and mess up my happy home? Didn't she know he was a married man? I've never seen him take off his ring. Not even now. I was filled with a poisonous hatred for her—whoever she was, I knew I could never forgive her for what she had done to us.

After all that, I couldn't very well <u>not</u> go to church with my family (despite the crappy things bubbling inside of me). But it's like we went through this ugly battle together and I didn't want to make any more waves. Besides, Aunt Stephie was being so helpful and supportive about everything, I figured it couldn't hurt to just play along.

But what was really surprising was that I actually liked her church. I mean it was kind of weird meeting in a grade school gymnasium without any pews or stained glass windows or organ playing. But their music was pretty cool, and the people <u>did</u> seem to be real, and I think they were actually glad to be there. Most of them seemed younger than the people at my regular church (not that age should matter that much—but it did make me curious). Even the pastor (who seems fairly young for a pastor) said some pretty good stuff that got me to really thinking. And, who knows, I just might go back there with Aunt Steph (that is if she keeps on going). Or maybe I'll even go back there on my own (now wouldn't that be weird!). But not next weekend. Because I'm still planning to go on the ski retreat and both Mom and Aunt Steph think it's a great idea. I'm pretty sure they're both worried about my soul being lost forever or something.

EIGHT

March 1, Thursday (Aunt Stephie's little "sex talk")

Somehow, for most of this week, I have managed not to mention the ski retreat to Jenny, and now there's only one day left and then I'm home free. It's not so much that I'm trying to be sneaky (at least that's what I keep telling myself) but I just don't see the point in telling her. I mean, Jenny and I are good friends and all (maybe even best friends) but I don't tell her <u>everything</u> about my life. I didn't tell her that I went to my aunt's church last Sunday. So, why should I tell her about this?

But I must confess, each time I see Josh (and usually he's with Jenny) my heart starts to pound a little harder and my palms get kind of sweaty. But not so that anyone would notice. I've gotten pretty good at playing it cool the last couple of months. I think I could even do pretty well at playing poker without giving anything away these days.

Beanie would be proud of my newly acquired skills. Of course, she never even glances my way anymore. I hardly ever see her at all anyway. But I did notice she's been hanging with a new boy—and actually he's not bad looking (tall and dark) but he dresses sort of weird (not unlike Beanie). I guess they make a pretty good pair.

Anyway, last night, Aunt Stephie took me to the mall to get a couple of things for the ski weekend (she's loaning me her skis and stuff like that) but she thought I still needed something new to wear. And so she bought me this really cool sweater that was on sale (since all the spring and summer clothes are out now). I've decided that Stephie has really changed. For one thing, she's a lot more thoughtful than she used to be. More generous too. Maybe it's her new church, or just maturity finally kicking in, but whatever it is I definitely like it.

Afterwards, we got some frozen yogurt and sat down for a while to talk. And suddenly I was telling her everything about Josh and Jenny and even the time Josh gave me a ride and I thought he was going to kiss me. It was like I was this bottle of soda that someone had just shook up and then opened! I just kept gushing all this stuff out while Stephie just quietly listened. But I wasn't too worried about her overreacting. I mean, she has all sorts of experience with guys and romance and stuff. And this is nothing compared to some of the things she's been through. Anyway, I really hoped she might actually have some words of encouragement for me. You know, something like: Hey, it's a free country, Caitlin; if you like Josh that much, then just go for it, girl!

But, as fate would have it, Stephie, being on her new religious kick right now, which even seems to have infiltrated into her brain (at least where relationships with guys are concerned) pulls a fast one on me. "You know, Caitlin," she begins carefully, as if measuring each word. "If I could go back and do my younger days all over again, I would definitely do everything a lot differently. For one thing, I made a bunch of mistakes with guys—and quite frankly, I'm the last person on the planet that you should be asking for advice on relationships."

Fine with me, I'm thinking and right then and there, I start to tell her to forget all about it, but before I can she continues. "But on the other hand, I guess I have learned a few things—the hard way, of course. And if there's one thing I've really changed my opinion on it's that sex should be confined within a marriage—"

"Okay," I say, holding up my hands to stop her. "I really don't need another sex talk, thank you very much."

Then she laughs. "No, that's not what this is supposed to be. I'm just saying that having done it all wrong, I can see now why it's really better to wait."

I just shake my head hopelessly. "Steph, why are you telling me all this? I mean, it's not like I'm planning to tackle Josh into some big snowdrift and just do it right there at the youth group retreat! Anyway, he's still going with my best friend."

She just smiles then (an obnoxious sort of smile which makes me feel even more uneasy than when she was actually talking) and she says, "I'm sure you'll make much better choices than I did, Caitlin. You're a lot smarter than I was when I was your age. And, hey, I'm sorry that I made you uncomfortable."

Relieved that <u>that</u> little chat is over, I gladly change the subject, and she begins giving me some skiing tips (since I've only been a couple of times before and I'd rather not make a total fool of myself). I know she was just trying to help, and I won't hold it against her.

March 4, Sunday (after the ski retreat)

<u>What a weekend</u>! I'm not even sure where to begin, but I think I need to get all this written down so I can begin to figure the whole thing out for myself because my head's still spinning.

First off, Josh sat next to me in the van on the way up to the resort, and we talked and talked. And it was so totally cool. Then, on the first night up there, (after we ate dinner and played a bunch of goofy, but fun, games) the youth pastor got everyone together in front of this big stone fireplace with a big crackling fire, and he said some really good stuff. In fact, he said some things that really challenged me to look at my own life in ways I'd never even considered (and it reminded me a lot of the way Pastor Tony at Steph's church talks). And for the first time since I can remember, things about God and faith really started making some sense. He said that to follow God is a conscious choice (not something you're just born into like belonging to the same church for as long as you can remember). But that you have to give up your-self entirely—and you have to surrender your whole life to God's son, Jesus Christ. And that only <u>then</u> can you have a personal relationship—and how that <u>relationship</u> will be more real and lasting than any other relationship, and how relationship is more important than religion. Now, I've never heard that before, and suddenly I'm thinking, that's what's wrong with my thinking—I've been looking for some religion to be all perfect and everything, but I don't even have a personal relationship with God.

Anyway, it was a lot to think about, but I was willing to consider it. That night Josh and several of us stayed up late talking with the youth pastor about all this stuff. It was really starting to make sense to me. It's like I could actually feel something happening inside me that was really different than anything I'd experienced at church before. And I'm not talking about the way you feel when you're thinking about a boy or anything like that. I mean something a whole lot bigger and better—something so promising and fulfilling that I can't even begin to describe it in words. <u>But it was there</u>. I know it was, and I was starting to feel really hopeful about my life and God and everything.

By the next day, I really wanted to hear more about how I could have this kind of relationship with God, and I had a feeling I was on the brink of discovering something amazing and life changing. But then something else amazing and life changing happened to me.

Well, Josh and I spent the <u>entire</u> day together. And by the second or third lift up the mountain, he was putting his arm around me. At first I thought he's just being sweet and friendly; like that kind of brotherly love that you always hear about in church. Because during all this time we're talking about God and how we can have a relationship with Jesus and how our lives are really changing, and all sorts of exciting things like that. But one time I was skiing down a fairly steep hill and took this really tight turn going too fast and ended up splattered all over the side of the hill, skis and poles everywhere. Anyway, Josh helped me get it all together, then helped me back into my skis and on to my feet. And then after he gently brushed the snow out of my hair and face, he put his arms around me and then solidly <u>kissed me</u>!

Well, let me tell you—it was quite a kiss! It felt like the whole mountain was spinning and shaking by the time he got done (and it was a fairly long kiss). Then all I could do was look up at him in utter amazement.

"What was that all about?" I managed to say (at least that's what I think I said), and he just laughed and said, "It's just because you are one very special girl, Caitlin O'Conner."

Well, have you ever been in an old house (like where my grandma lives not too far from Beanie's house) and all the electricity goes through this one little fuse box out on the back porch. If you plug in too many electrical appliances the fuse box just blows up and you see all these flashes and smoke, and then all the lights go out, and you have to go get a flashlight and replace the blown out fuses? I guess that's sort of how I felt about then. Way too much was going on inside me. It's like I was this overloaded fuse box about to blow up.

But because Josh was right there with me, and God (though closer than ever before) seemed farther away, I just decided to plug all my circuits into Josh, figuring I could think about God later (he's always available, right?). So Josh and I spent all our free time together. And yes, we kissed—we kissed a lot! I can hardly explain exactly how it felt when we kissed (and maybe it's stupid to write about such things, but I just don't think I can help myself because it was so totally incredible!). Anyway, it's sort of like the air gets sucked right out of my chest and my stomach does flip-flops and my brain tingles. I know, that makes it sound sort of gross and unpleasant. Believe me, it was anything but unpleasant! Actually, it was totally magical!

All I wanted to do was to be with Josh, to feel his arms wrapped around me, and to lock lips with him forever and ever! I'm more certain than ever that I'm totally and irrevocably and hopelessly in love.

I'm just not sure how we're going to break all this to Jenny. I figure it's Josh's problem. After all, he's the one who's going with her, he's the one who should break it up, right? And even though I feel totally guilty about it (and believe me I really do), I know it's all for the best to break the news quickly and get it over with. Because how could Josh possibly love Jenny as much as he loves me? Sure I know that Josh and Jenny went all the way and everything (and I'm still not real happy about that). But the way I see it, that's a big part of their problem.

But, Josh has changed now. He's trying to live like a Christian (and so am I). And he and I can have a really good relationship without going all the way. At least I'm pretty sure we can—although there were a couple of times when we were kissing and touching, and I did wonder—what <u>would</u> it be like? But I'm sure we'd never do <u>that</u>. I'm not ready for anything like that, yet. And Josh said himself that he wants to live differently now (and I'm pretty sure <u>that's</u> what he was talking about). The youth pastor discussed all that boy-girl stuff on Saturday night. Not that I heard all that much since Josh had his arm around me and all I could think about was the strength in his shoulders and the warmth of his body. But I'm fairly certain things are going to be different between Josh and me than they were with him and Jenny.

I'm just worried about what this is going to do to my friendship with Jenny. And even though I'm willing to sacrifice our friendship in order to be Josh Miller's girlfriend, it really will make me sad to hurt her like this. I'll miss her friendship (although I don't think we were ever really best friends—not the way it was with Beanie and me). But anyway when Jenny realizes how happy Josh and I are together—and how right the whole thing is—I'm sure she'll forgive us, in time.

March 5, Monday (the waiting game)

I tried to avoid Jenny today. I just couldn't look her in the eyes. She noticed I had a little sunburn on my face (from the ski trip) and asked how I'd gotten that since it had been cloudy in town all weekend. I just laughed and said, "Didn't you know I flew off to the Bahamas last Friday?" That seemed to satisfy her. And then I hurried off to class.

I hardly caught a glimpse of Josh all day, although I wasn't really too worried. The truth is, I was still flying so high from our weekend that I almost didn't mind. I knew our time would come, and besides I wasn't sure if he'd had a chance to break the news to Jenny yet. So I didn't go out of my way to find him. But finally when school was over, I looked all around and didn't see him anywhere and that bothered me a little. Then I noticed Jenny was gone too, and that's when I realized—he must be telling her now. So I just rode the bus home. I didn't even see Beanie on the bus and I sat by myself and daydreamed about how fun the ski weekend had been.

Then I got home, and here I have stayed all afternoon, just waiting for the phone to ring, and for Josh to tell me the whole story of how it went with Jenny. But now it's eleven o'clock at night, and he still hasn't called. I'm feeling just a little worried. I'd considered calling him, but I always think that's kind of pathetic when a girl calls a guy. I'm sure that's a pretty archaic way of thinking (not to mention unliberated) and I may get over it in time. But right now I'd much rather Josh call me than for me to call him. I guess I'll just have to talk to him tomorrow. I've already picked out a really cool outfit to wear. I just hope Jenny doesn't want to kill me or anything real messy.

NINE

March 6, Tuesday (dead dogs and broken hearts)

When I saw Jenny by the lockers this morning, I could tell right off she was upset and had been crying recently, and so naturally I tried to escape without being seen by her. But it was too late.

She called out to me, and what could I do? So, I go over and she immediately begins telling me about how her golden retriever, Dolly, was hit by a car yesterday and later died at the vet clinic. Now, I've always liked Dolly and had even asked Mom if I could get a dog just like her, so, like Jenny, I began to cry too, which Jenny thinks is very sweet. We hug and everything, and then I realize that Josh must not have told her about us yet (probably in light of her loss), for which I am greatly relieved. It's bad enough to lose your dog, but not your boyfriend too. So I decide just to play it cool and wait until Jenny has a chance to get over this loss.

But when Jenny gave me a ride home from school just an hour or so ago, she said that the only thing that got

her through losing Dolly was Josh, and how she felt closer
to him now than ever before. Of course, I didn't know
what to say, but I did feel extremely curious, so I asked,
"Was Josh there when it happened?" She said yes, and
that it was Josh who had actually found Dolly and then
how the two of them rushed her to the vet, and when
Dolly died it was Josh who held Jenny and comforted her.
Well, I guess I can understand that—I mean, what do you
do when someone's dog dies like that?

What I <u>cannot</u> understand (or even believe for that
matter) is the next thing Jenny said. And actually, I hope
with all my heart that she is lying. But then why would
she lie?

Jenny then told me that after Josh brought her home,
he continued to "comfort" her and the next thing she
knew they were up in her room making out. Her mom came
home early and Josh actually jumped right out her window, which she seemed to think was pretty hilarious! Well,
I think I could've just died right there in Jenny's car (and
not because Josh landed in the rosebush!), but fortunately we were at my house by then, and I managed to
thank her and get out and find my way to the front
door before I collapsed inside. Now I feel like someone has
rammed a huge dagger right into my chest and is twist-
ing it!

Can what she said possibly be true? Why would Josh
do something like that to me? And even though I've been
in my room crying for the last hour, I'm still hoping that it's
a horrible, horrible lie. I've decided that if Josh doesn't

call me, I <u>will</u> call him. At least I think I will. I'm not totally sure. In fact, I'm not sure about anything right now, except that I'm in pain. <u>Severe pain</u>. If what Jenny said is true, I want to know: How do you live through something like this?

And can I?

(later that same evening)

I cannot bring myself to call Josh. I cannot bear to sound so totally pitiful as to call him and ask if this is true. <u>Why hasn't he called me</u>? It makes me think that it must be true! And if it's true, how can I live? How can I see him at school and say nothing? How can I pretend that nothing ever happened between us? And how can I continue to be friends with Jenny Lambert? If what she said is true, I feel like I hate her—hate her with my whole heart.

I think I hate myself too.

Life is too miserable.

March 7, Wednesday (my darkest hour)

My life is over. Absolutely over. And I am <u>not</u> just being melodramatic. It is over. Completely over.

I did it. Today, I confronted Josh about this whole stupid mess—and right in the middle of everything Jenny walked up from behind. And without me knowing it, she stood there and listened to me go on. I don't even think I really care that she heard a lot of what I said (at least she's seeing a side of Josh she maybe wasn't aware of). It was an awful scene. Jenny started yelling and Josh said absolutely nothing! I can't even bring myself to write down all the details of it right now.

Suffice it to say that I truly wish I were dead and that my life would be over, completely over. I've never been the type of person to seriously consider suicide (and even as I write those words it sounds a little crazy), but the truth is I've had those thoughts today. It would be such an easy escape just to have everything be all over with. It would finally stop this pain that is devouring my heart like a fast-acting cancer. What I wouldn't do just to make it all end.

I think I could've withstood the public humiliation when Jenny tore into me in front of (what I had just begun to think of as) my friends (but who, of course, no longer are). And I could have lived through losing Jenny's friendship (which has without a doubt occurred today). But what is killing me more than any of this is that <u>Josh has chosen Jenny over me</u>. It's just that simple.

I am yesterday's news (without ever making the news). He has picked Jenny (the cheerleader) Lambert over Caitlin (the nobody) O'Conner.

Even after all that happened and all he said last weekend (only three days ago—and yet it seems like another lifetime) he has turned his back completely on me as if I were nothing more than a moment's entertainment, and he has chosen Jenny. And, yes, by the way, they did do it in her bedroom just like she told me. At least Jenny isn't a liar.

I wonder if it hurts to die. Surely, it cannot hurt any

more than to live like this. And I'm certain that I can never show my face in school again. I wonder if I could transfer over to McFadden. Or maybe do homeschool.

I know that Mom's really worried about me. She knows that I came home from school before lunchtime, and then barricaded myself in my room all day (teachers have some special network for these things), and even Benjamin has begged me to come out and eat something. Aunt Stephie came over to talk to me. But I just cannot talk to anyone right now. I keep telling them, I just need to be alone to think (like Dad says, to figure things out).

Maybe if I stay up here long enough, I can simply die from a natural cause like starvation. Or perhaps it's actually possible to die from a broken heart. Surely the pain is enough to kill you.

God, are you still there? Can you even hear me? Did you make all this happen to me? Do you even care?

TEN

March 16, Friday (I survived)

I know, it's been a long, long while since I've written anything in my diary. I guess that's because I've been living in the black abyss these past two weeks. Somehow I made it to school for the rest of that hopelessly awful week (after I made such a fool of myself).

I wore black and kept my head down low and spoke to no one. Even Beanie tried to talk to me, but I just snapped at her and told her to mind her own business. I knew Jenny and her friends (and probably everyone else) were all talking about me behind my back, whispering as I passed them in the halls. Somehow it didn't really seem to matter all that much. Not compared to the hurt I felt inside about Josh. Somehow, I have managed not to see him for nearly two weeks. Maybe God is watching over me, just a little, after all. Now that it's spring break, I have a whole week without having to slink down a hall-way trying to avoid almost everyone.

I think the biggest miracle is that I'm still alive (and I'm not kidding). But the fact is: I am. And although I feel like I'm a totally different person, I have survived this. I guess that's okay that I'm different. I think maybe I needed to change. But changing like that sure hurts. I don't think I could go through too much more of it. I suppose it's true what they say about time healing all wounds—although at the rate I'm going it may take a couple more years to get just partially over this. According to Aunt Stephie, God is there and he's ready to help. Maybe he's helping me already. I'm just not sure.

It has occurred to me that I may have made a big mistake on that ski retreat weekend (okay, maybe <u>several</u> mistakes), but there's one that I think is bigger than the rest. I think I made the mistake of choosing Josh over God. At the time it seemed right to me— probably because it felt so good. But I am questioning where my life might be right now if I'd chosen differently. And I'm wondering if it's too late to undo it. Oh, of course, I know I can't undo what I've done with my "popular" so-called friends or with Josh. None of them will talk to me anymore. To tell you the truth I don't even care.

I think Beanie noticed that something has changed in me, and despite the fact that I bit her head off a week or so ago, she has surprisingly (or not) been reaching out to me again. But now I feel so bad about the way I treated her that I am almost afraid to talk to her.

Although, I finally did agree to see her this weekend. I'm just not sure what I'll say.

I suppose I should begin with "I'm sorry."

March 17, Saturday (Beanie's back)

Beanie came over today. It was so good to spend time with her again. What could I have been thinking these last three months when I shut her out of my life? What a stupid, shallow person I have been! Beanie has more depth and character and intelligence in her little finger than all those "popular" kids put together. I don't know how I missed that.

Well, right off the bat, I told her how sorry I was about all that nonsense, and Beanie (being Beanie) just totally forgave me. Then she told me about what's been going on with her of late. Her new friend (and she implicitly stated that he's <u>not</u> her boyfriend) moved here from Seattle right after the new year (they met in journalism class). His name is Zach Streeter and apparently he's a very committed Christian. This interested me a lot, and so I asked her quite a bit about it. As it turns out, she considers herself to be a real Christian as well now. She told me that it's different than when she used to go to the youth group with me, that now she has actually "accepted Jesus Christ as her personal Savior" (her own words) and that her life hasn't been the same since.

Then I told her about what I'd heard at the ski retreat and how close I'd come to doing the exact same thing—but how I'd gotten somewhat derailed by a stupid boy (and of course I then had to tell her that whole pitiful tale). But oddly enough, I felt just a teeny bit better after telling her; it made the whole thing seem slightly less significant somehow.

Anyway, she told me that she and Zach are still looking for a good church to go to (his family doesn't go to church and she's not too impressed with my old church). I told her a little about Aunt Steph's church, and she said it sounded interesting and maybe they would both come to visit tomorrow. Then we went to the mall and met Zach there, and we all went to a funny movie together. And for the first time in two weeks, it felt like I was almost having fun.

Afterwards we went out for ice cream and somehow Zach talked us both into going out for track! I still can't believe that I agreed, but Beanie and I used to do track together in middle school (and we weren't half bad either—she was a good sprinter and I did long jump, high jump, and some of the longer distance runs). Zach is really into track and he told us we should give it a try, and that way the three of us can hang together this spring. Actually, that sounds kind of good to me, because to tell you the truth the last couple weeks have been pretty bleak and lonely (and that's a total understatement). So I guess I will give it a try. Zach said we have to come to practice every day during spring break, starting on Monday (and now I'm wondering if I'm even good enough to make the team).

When I got home tonight, my mom was waiting up for me. She wanted to know how I was doing, and I thought maybe I should finally tell her a little about what's going on in my life. And the amazing thing is we stayed up really late talking about all this stuff (of course I didn't tell her everything!) but it was kind of fun. We even talked about Dad a little. I guess he called again this week and thinks maybe he wants to come home. But my mom (and this surprises me) said she told him maybe she didn't want <u>him</u> anymore (and I'll bet that surprised him even more!). Anyway, I guess Dad has almost convinced her that he still hasn't actually cheated on her (other than in his heart) and some of his old Bible study buddies have been talking to him and encouraging him to come back to us.

But I don't think my mom's ready for him to return yet. And I think that's okay. Quite frankly, I don't mind seeing him squirm a little. I just hope she doesn't wait too long because you never know what that Belinda person might do. I mean, my dad is pretty good looking (for an older guy) and who knows how desperate this chick may be. I'll stand by Mom in whatever she chooses to do. She said we'll do some fun things this week for spring break, although we can't spend too much money (I think she's getting a little worried about finances and the possibility of being a single mom).

March 18, Sunday

We went to Aunt Steph's church again today. I guess I'll have to quit calling it Aunt Steph's church (it's really called Faith Fellowship) and the pastor's name is Tony

Berringer and today his younger brother, Clay, started
leading a youth group, which was handy since Beanie
and Zach also showed up today. Clay's only eighteen and
still in high school himself (a senior) but he seems really
mature and a natural born leader. He goes to the crosstown rival high school (McFadden), but we don't hold that
against him. It doesn't hurt that he's not too difficult to
look at (not that I'm into that sort of thing these days!).
There were only about ten of us in the group, and most of
the kids (other than we three) are from McFadden, but
they seem pretty nice. As Beanie pointed out it seems like
they're there because they want to be, not because
their parents have dragged them kicking and screaming.
It was a pretty good time. But to be honest, I felt a little
out of place because I'm fairly certain (by what was
said) that everyone in that group has a personal relationship with Jesus Christ. Everyone but me. I figure I should
be able to remedy that situation. It seems like it's just
about time (or maybe way overdue, now that I think
about it!).

And so I am going to do something totally unprece-
dented (at least in my life). Tonight (March 18) in the
privacy of my own room, I am going to pray and invite
Jesus Christ to come into my heart, and I'm going to ask
him to become my personal Savior (and, man, do I need
one!).

I have decided that just because I totally blew it at
the ski retreat doesn't mean that God won't give me a
second chance (in fact, Clay was talking about second

chances today). I can't think of any reason a person can't do this sort of thing privately. I mean, I'll be happy to tell anyone who wants to know all about everything later on. But it seems to me that making this kind of a commitment is kind of a personal sort of thing, and I'm certain that it's no less meaningful if I do it right here and now without anyone but God watching.

(about an hour later)

Okay, I did it! And to tell the truth I didn't feel any different (at least not at first). I wondered if maybe I did something wrong (like maybe you have to use just certain words or something). So now I'll write down what I prayed (as best I can remember and I admit it probably wasn't the way they'd do it in church). But I basically said:

"God, if you're really, really there, and you can actually hear me, and if you really want to have a relationship with me, I'm pretty sure I'd like to have a relationship with you. And so, right now, I'd like to invite Jesus Christ into my heart. I know I've done all kinds of cruddy stuff and you might not even want me, but that's not what I hear from everyone else—they say you'll take <u>anyone</u>. So, right now, I'm asking you to come into my heart. And maybe you can somehow make something of my life. I've sure made enough messes of it myself." Then I said, "Amen."

I guess that's about all I said. I know it wasn't a very pretty prayer, but I really did mean every word, and somehow I think <u>that's</u> what counts.

Well then, slowly, I began to feel something sort of growing inside me (I honestly don't think it was my imagination either). It was this feeling that was sort of warm and comforting (like drinking hot cocoa after being out in the cold—only lots, lots better), and then deep peace (you know, like when you let out a big, long sigh of relief and you know that everything is going to be okay). And then I got the strongest sense that God really does love me! It was so exciting and encouraging. I mean, I wasn't really sure he would actually love me—especially when I've done some pretty stupid things lately and all. But somehow I know that he does! And I feel really good—not to mention relieved!

When I realized that God loves me, I started to get this amazing feeling of joy, like it was bubbling right up inside of me. I know I can't be making that part up, because I haven't felt anything even remotely related to joy for the past two weeks (anyone can tell you that!).

And so, I really believe this is for real. I really believe that Jesus is in my heart—right now! And it's pretty exciting! I really didn't expect to feel this happy—it seems like just last week I wanted to die. But now I'm looking forward to living—and having Jesus living inside me! This is really great! I'm going to have to tell someone about this—and soon! It's too much to keep inside. It's just soooo great!

But now I'm wondering if this all means that I'll have to start thinking and doing a lot of things differently. You know, become a better person somehow. I've heard Clay say that Jesus will help us to change. Man, will I need help.

Anyway, this is definitely a day to remember—and I know it's a real turning point in my life. I can't wait to tell Clay!

I'm going to call Beanie and tell her the amazing news—I bet she'll be shocked! And then, even though it's not even ten o'clock yet, I'll go right to bed and hopefully sleep (because I have to get up early since track practice starts at seven in the morning tomorrow). I just hope I can make the team now, and I wonder if God could help me out there? I guess it can't hurt to ask.

OH, THANK YOU, GOD! THANK YOU FOR LOVING AND FORGIVING ME! AND THANK YOU FOR COMING INTO MY HEART! AMEN AND AMEN!

ELEVEN

March 19, Monday (my first day as a real Christian)

Mom let me drive her car to the school to try out for track this morning. I prayed all the way there (not for my driving, but just because I was so happy to have God living inside me!). Then when I showed up for track practice, Mr. Reynolds (the coach) said that Beanie and I could warm up and practice with the team (who had already been practicing for a week or so) and then he'd give us both official tryouts (I think he's impressed that Zach put in a good word for us).

I practiced my high jump and long jump and then ran a few laps. And then Mr. Reynolds (after timing Beanie in a couple of sprints which she managed to pull off just fine!) came over to check out my jumping abilities. I must admit I was surprised that I could still jump at all, but just the same I wasn't too sure if I was good enough to make the team (and suddenly, more than anything, I really wanted to!). So as I was standing on the turf staring at the high-jump bar (set pretty low to start with), I began to pray (not for any superpower ability, but just that I wouldn't be too nervous, and that I'd do my best) and then I began to jump.

Well, let me tell you, I just kept sailing right over that bar better than I'd ever done before until Mr. Reynolds finally set it at five feet! And I think that kind of threw me off, and then I couldn't clear it anymore. Disappointed, I walked over to him, ready to hear the sad news that I hadn't made the team. But instead he just shook my hand and said, "Welcome to the team." He didn't even ask to see my long jump or whether I could run or not (which I'm thinking I might prefer not to do). I know it seems kind of silly on my part, but I was so happy I almost cried. Almost!

Then Zach and Beanie and I went out for burgers at lunchtime to celebrate making the team, and I told them about how I actually prayed before jumping, and then I even told Zach about how I'd asked Jesus into my heart last night. Both of them were so excited about the whole thing. I couldn't believe how much better I feel being friends with these guys than I ever did with Jenny and the rest of the bunch.

I guess maybe sometimes you just need to sample some unpleasant things to understand how much better the other things are.

March 23, Friday (a very good week)

I know it seems incredible, and I can hardly believe it
myself, but this has been one of the best weeks of my
entire life! It's especially amazing when I consider how less
than three weeks ago, I was seriously considering suicide
as an answer to my messed up life. But I think, even then,
that God was protecting me.

THANK YOU, GOD, FOR WATCHING OVER ME EVEN WHEN
I DIDN'T REALIZE YOU WERE THERE.

Track practice has been great all week (hard work
and sore muscles, but worth it). And as it turns out, Coach
Reynolds is a Christian (I think that's part of the reason
Zach wanted us to come out for track); anyway, he's a
nice coach and really encouraging. And our little team is
pretty good too (although I heard some of the kids are
gone this week because of spring break). But I really feel
like I'm fitting in with everyone on the team, and getting
to know some new kids.

Nathan Parker (remember, my Valentine's Dance
date) is on the team too (he throws discus and shot put),
and he actually said hi to me today. I said hi back, but
nothing else. Not that I'm trying to be unfriendly, but
somehow I don't really care if I don't have anything to do
with that particular group of kids anymore. It's like this
big heavy weight has been lifted off me just knowing
that I'll never have to perform for those kids again. Let
me tell you, it's so much better just being myself and
hanging with people like Beanie and Zach (especially

more so now that I have a relationship with God—which keeps getting better, by the way!).

And things have even gotten better on the home front too. Tonight (of all things) my dad has actually invited my mom to go out on a <u>date</u> with him. Pretty funny. But she agreed, making no promises for anything more than just dinner. I'm glad she's going though. I was starting to get worried that her resistance might actually push Dad straight into Belinda's arms. The truth is, I'd like to see my family get back together, eventually. Even now, I'm working on forgiving Dad (although it's not easy). He's even called and talked to me a couple of times now where I haven't actually hung up on him.

I thought about telling him that I became a Christian, but somehow I couldn't do it. The timing didn't seem right. But I will, eventually. Maybe I need to totally forgive him first. To be honest, I'm having a hard time with that. But like Zach keeps saying about track and stuff, "all things are possible with God." (Actually I think he got that from the Bible, but it's a good promise just the same!)

March 25, Sunday (last day of spring break)

I almost hate for spring break to end. It's been so fun (and relaxing not having to be at school). But I think I'm a lot stronger and ready to face things again (Jenny et al). I feel like I've really grown this week and I think I can actually walk through the halls holding my head up (not in pride, but just without the old humiliation).

Okay, I'll admit that it probably doesn't hurt any that I just got my hair cut (and it looks pretty good—not that I think looks are that big of a deal!). My dad took Benjamin and me to the mall this afternoon (after church) and bought us some things. I got a few new items of clothing which might help bolster my confidence. But let me make this perfectly clear—I am not ever going to turn into that shallow girl I used to be! Still, it's fun to look nice; and I'm pretty sure it's not a sin. I mean, just look at all the beautiful green leaves and flowers starting to bloom around us and you have to know that God appreciates beauty too!

So, anyway, I'm ready to go to school with Jesus in my heart and a whole new outlook. And if I see Jenny and her bunch making fun of me, well, I'll just smile their way and forgive them and keep minding my own business. Maybe someday I'll even get a chance to tell them how God can make their lives a whole lot more fulfilling!

March 26, Monday (an unhappy discovery)

Just when I think my life has taken a huge turn for the better (and not to say things aren't greatly improved with God in my life) it just figures that life can never be completely perfect. Still I'm determined that I am not going to let this get me down.

Okay, here's what happened. After a fairly decent day (where I could actually walk down the halls without feeling like total scum, and telling myself that I belong to God, and refusing to worry about what Jenny and her

clique may or may not be saying) I go down to the girls'
locker room with Beanie and I'm sort of rejoicing that I
made it through this day. And so we get all dressed
down for track and jog out to the field, where it's sunny
and nice, and who's the first person I see warming up on
the track?

None other than Josh Miller, all ready for practice. (It
turns out he's on the track team but had been out of
town during spring break!) Well, my eyes just about popped
out of my head when I saw him there stretching out his
calf muscles. My first instinct was to just quit the team,
right then and there. In fact, I actually froze in my steps,
turned around, and started to head straight back to
the locker room. But Beanie chased me down, and with
the help of Zach (who was just coming out), they managed to talk me out of quitting.

So they walked me over to the high jump pit (like I
was crippled or something) and there the two of them
stuck by my side, practically holding my hand, until I
regained enough composure to start doing some warm-ups.
Naturally, Zach didn't know anything about what had
gone on between Josh and me, and so Beanie quickly
gave him the lowdown. Then Zach informed us that Josh
was Harrison High's star runner. (Or rather, had been for
the past few years, but it seemed that a certain new-
comer from Seattle planned on giving that Miller boy a
run for his money!) Since starting high school, neither
Beanie nor I had ever paid that much attention to the
track team, so this was news to us.

Now I'm thinking maybe it's a good thing that I didn't know, for I never would've joined the team. Even now, I'm almost wishing that I hadn't. But like Beanie says, "It's not fair to let a selfish, two-timing boy frighten you away from something that you really want to do." I <u>do</u> want to stay on the team, and by the end of last week my jumping had really improved, Coach Reynolds even said so. I just wish Josh Miller would suddenly sprain an ankle or something (okay, that's probably wrong of me, but I just wish he didn't have to be around to spoil everything for me!). And just when it seemed I was getting over him. Will I ever get over him?

DEAR GOD, PLEASE HELP ME. I WANT TO FORGET THAT I EVER CARED FOR JOSH MILLER. BUT I THINK I'M GOING TO NEED SOME EXTRA HELP. CAN YOU PLEASE LEND A HAND?

March 29, Thursday (judge not?)

A weird thing happened tonight. I'm still not sure what it all means, but I know I need to give it some more thought. It all started when Zach took Beanie and me to the mall after practice tonight. (Beanie and I had decided we needed to get new track shoes for our first meet, which is tomorrow, by the way).

And since (only by the grace of God, I'm sure) I've managed to stay on the track team without having to actually speak to Josh (although I'm pretty sure I caught him looking at me at least twice). Somehow that makes me feel slightly better to know that he's looking, because then I get some satisfaction out of completely ignoring him. It might not be the nicest thing to do, but under the circumstances, I think it's somewhat understandable. But let me get to the weird thing that happened tonight.

After Beanie and I bought our shoes (Zach, by the way, was very knowledgeable in helping us make the best choices), we decided to grab a pizza at this new place right next to the mall (we figured we'd start storing up our carbos for tomorrow's meet, and I still had a few bucks from my dad, so I offered to treat). So, we're all sitting happily in a booth, and I happen to look up and see my dad sitting just a couple booths away, but he doesn't notice me.

Well, I figure the proper thing would be to get up to go say hello. After all, he and Mom seemed to have had a pretty good time on their "date" last weekend. And he's been calling her every night. I'm walking over there and he looks up and sees me, but he gets this sort of horrified look on his face, and suddenly I realize what's up. <u>He is there with Belinda!</u>

Now I'm just a few feet away and I don't know what to do. Should I turn around and go back? By then my dad's recovered enough to wave me over to his table, smiling as if it's the most normal thing in the world to have your daughter catch you eating dinner with "the other woman." So I continue to his table, thinking maybe I'm wrong, maybe he's just with a business acquaintance (I mean I've never seen the woman before). But no, he introduces her as Belinda Lithgow. And I note right off that she is 1) sort of youngish (maybe in her twenties) 2) a pretty redhead, and 3) looking at my dad like he's Mr. Wonderful!

Well, it's more than I can handle and I just abruptly walk away without even saying how do you do? or good-bye or anything. When I get back to my table, Beanie and Zach notice immediately that something is definitely wrong. My hands are shaking and I'm close to tears. But we've already ordered our pizza so I know we can't just leave. I explain what happened and the two of them are sympathetic and supportive, and by the time our pizza arrives, my dad and his "girlfriend" are leaving.

Now, I'm getting all angry and furious, and I start to bluster about this Belinda chick, saying, "How can she do this? She knows he's married and yet she's willing to break up our whole family just to have him," and lots of angry stuff like that.

Finally, Beanie reaches over and puts her hand on my shoulder and says, "Maybe you shouldn't be so hard on her, Caitlin. I mean, remember when you went after Josh Miller knowing full well that he and Jenny were still together?" Well, that sure shut me up fast. Not that I greatly appreciate Beanie's comparison (and it's not like Josh and Jenny were married), but then again I guess she does make a valid point. Thankfully, Zach changes the subject, and I decide not to hold anything against Beanie—even if it did hurt my feelings a little. (I know we're supposed to keep forgiving each other. We talked about that in youth group last week—seven times seventy—which is supposed to stand for infinity or something really huge like that.)

Now I'm sitting here in my room, thinking about how Beanie was probably right. I mean, I suppose I was a little bit like Belinda. And, man, if that doesn't make me feel lower than dirt. To think that Belinda and I actually have such a despicable thing in common is truly a shock to the system (not to mention totally humiliating). I guess I shouldn't judge her so much. I still don't feel like I can forgive her—I don't even know if I can forgive Dad. To tell you the truth, all this forgiveness business has me just a little bit worried.

Of course that reminds me that I need to forgive myself too. Clay talked about that in youth group. He said if we don't forgive ourselves, it can be really hard to receive God's forgiveness (not to mention forgiving others). But now (big painful groan!) I'm also wondering if I don't need to ask Jenny Lambert to forgive me. And anything would be easier than _that_. I cannot, for the life of me, imagine crawling back to Jenny to apologize for what it feels like _they_ did to me. Wasn't I sort of the victim there? Or maybe not. I don't know for sure. Beanie's comments paint this whole picture in a brand new light, and I don't like what I'm seeing. Maybe it's like they say: The truth hurts.

PLEASE, GOD, SHOW ME WHAT TO DO. HELP ME TO FORGIVE ALL THESE PEOPLE (IF YOU WANT ME TO). MAYBE I DO NEED TO GO AND TALK TO JENNY, I'M JUST NOT SURE. PLEASE SHOW ME HOW AND WHEN TO DO IT. AND PLEASE,

HELP ME TO FORGIVE MYSELF FOR BEING THE "OTHER WOMAN" WHO TRIED TO COME BETWEEN JOSH AND JENNY. I CAN SEE NOW HOW WRONG THAT WAS. THANK YOU, I GUESS, FOR LETTING ME SEE MYSELF FOR WHAT I REALLY AM, EVEN IF I DON'T LIKE IT VERY MUCH. PLEASE HELP ME TO CHANGE. AMEN.

TWELVE

March 30, Friday (first track meet)

I think our first track meet went pretty well, and I mean on several levels. To start with, I placed first in high jump (I couldn't even believe it!). Then I placed third in long jump (only two inches behind the girl who won first). And then I got to shout and cheer as Zach took first place in every single one of his running events (with Josh coming in a fairly close second). But what was probably the highlight of this meet (for me) was when I was standing on the sidelines and spotted Jenny standing nearby (she was looking right at me), and suddenly I knew the time had come to go and say I'm sorry.

So, I just walked right up and did it. I could tell she was really shocked, and I halfway expected her to say or do something totally rude (I was even prepared to just take it). But amazingly enough she didn't.

She just sort of shrugged then said, "It's okay. I know it takes two to tango, and I hold Josh just as responsible as you." I mumbled a quick thanks then turned to go back to the field, but she grabbed my arm and stopped me. "Hey, Caitlin," she said, "we can still be friends, you know."

I tried to conceal my surprise at this and managed to nod and say, "Sure, I don't see why not." But at the same time I was thinking, <u>Thanks, but no thanks—been there done that!</u> Instead I just smiled and waved and went off in search of Beanie. I didn't tell Beanie what Jenny said. I think I've learned that you don't have to repeat every single little thing you hear. Like someone once said, Some things are just better left unsaid.

Just in case I'm starting to sound all saintly and good in my diary, I have a true confession to make. One of the happiest moments of the track meet today (besides winning first and then having Jenny forgive me) was when I saw the look of totally crushed disappointment wash across Josh's pretty face each time Zach creamed him in another race. Particularly in the 100 meters when Beanie and I were waiting right at the finish line, all ready to congratulate Zach. Josh just stared at the three of us as if we were all from another planet or something. I could just imagine him wondering, Just who do they think they are to rock my world like this?

I know it's wrong to take pleasure in another person's sufferings, but in all honesty I totally enjoyed seeing Josh beaten like that. So, you see, I'm not even close to perfect!

April 1, Sunday (who's fooling who?)

I never told my Mom about seeing Dad with Belinda at the pizza place on Thursday night. I figure it might just be another one of those things that's better left unsaid. But for some reason I feel really guilty about it, especially when Mom and Dad went out on another one of their little "dates" last night. Today Mom was in such great spirits, and then, after church, Benjamin and I were supposed to go do something with Dad again. This time I bailed, saying I had to do homework, and suggesting maybe it'd be better for them to just do a father-son kind of thing, and Ben didn't seem to mind a bit.

After they were gone, Mom asked me if something was up between me and my dad, and I had to lie to her and say no. And that makes me feel really rotten. So, I've decided to just confront my dad face to face (hopefully without getting all angry, since in youth group today Clay talked about how we should do everything in love, and even though it sounds impossible in this case, I'm sure Clay is probably right—he seems to understand these things better than anyone I know).

So, now my plan is to confront my dad and not forget that I love him (at least I think I do, or anyway, I used to). I asked him if we could do something together later on this week, and that seemed to make him happy, or maybe he was just relieved. I hope he doesn't think this means I'm going to cover for him about that Belinda thing, because if he does he's in for a big surprise. I've decided I will not lie to Mom for him anymore. I'll tell him that for him to continue seeing both Belinda and Mom is totally unfair, not to mention despicable. And even though I'm trying not to judge Belinda (due to what Beanie said), I still think what they're doing is completely wrong. And even if the Bible says I have to love and forgive them both, I'm certain that doesn't mean that I just accept what they're doing as all right.

April 5, Thursday (our second track meet presents a small dilemma)

We had our second track meet today. It was an away meet (about an hour's ride on a hot stinky bus). And then it rained at the meet, turning everything into a miserable muddy mess. I did lousy in long jump (kept slipping), but managed to place second in high jump (and Coach Reynolds told me the girl who took first went to state last year—and she only beat me by an inch!). So I was feeling okay as Beanie and I huddled under a soggy blanket and watched Zach taking first place in every one of his races again. (This time I actually tried _not_ to rejoice too greatly over Josh's losses, and I even told him good job for coming in _third_—okay, maybe I was gloating just a little.)

After the meet was over we all piled our wet and smelly bodies into the detestable bus. Beanie and Zach were already sitting together (no big deal) and so I grabbed the empty seat in front of them, and the next thing I know Josh Miller flops down <u>right beside me!</u> Now, it's a free country and people should be able to sit wherever they want on a bus (I think Rosa Parks established this!), but there were plenty of other seats for him to sit in (and plenty of willing people, especially girls, to share them with Josh), so I just don't see why he had to go and sit right next to me.

Completely ignoring him, I turned around and began talking to Beanie and Zach, going on quite extensively about how wonderful Zach had done in his events (I'm sure to Zach's embarrassment since he's really pretty humble about his athletic abilities). Then Josh, just as cool as you please, turns around and starts agreeing with me, congratulating Zach and asking all about his previous track records and stuff like that.

Well, let me tell you, I don't like Josh Miller sticking his nose into <u>my</u> little world. What right does he have to talk to <u>my</u> friends anyway? Finally, I just turned back around in my seat and stared out the fogged up window, and, I have to admit, sulked. Why was he doing this in the first place? Since when has Josh Miller cared about anyone but himself? Was he just trying to torture me? And if so, he was doing a really great job at it. But why? It was hard for me to believe that he really wanted to talk with Zach.

Then like a flash, it hits me—of course he wants to get to know Zach better. I mean, Zach Streeter is Harrison High's most promising track star at the moment. And stars like to know stars (it's like they're attracted to

the mutual light or something—probably just hoping it will
shine a little brighter on themselves!). So, anyway, I
decided that's what was going on: Josh was just trying to
get cozy with Zach so he'd look better. Okay, I guess I
can live with that. And so, I tried not to be too infuriated
as I sat there, leaning my head into the window, pretending to be asleep.

But then a totally disgusting thing happened.
Detestable! (I'm sure that's how Jane Austen would
describe it, and I've been reading her books again.) And,
sure, I have no one to blame for this but myself. (Well,
that and the fact that Josh's body is pressing close to
mine as he takes up more than half of the seat!) The
next thing, I realize that I'm thinking about him again, in
that way. Yes, as nauseating as it sounds, I start imagining him with his arm around me, kissing me, and everything! And I have to admit I did actually enjoy those
feelings (be it ever so briefly), but then the realization
hits me, and it just makes me sick! What is wrong with me?
How could I so easily fall into such stupidity?

Thankfully, the whole episode only lasted a few seconds. But it scared me just the same. I started to wonder if Josh might possibly have some sort of power he
could use over me (like a love potion). Now I know that's
totally ridiculous. At least I think it is. But just to be safe,
I'll try to keep more distance between us from now on.

But here's the part that's really bugging me about
this whole Josh Miller thing. When Zach took Beanie and
me home, he told us how he thinks Josh is, in his own words,

"spiritually searching." He went on about how he wants to get to know Josh better and share some stuff about Jesus with him. In no uncertain terms, I told Zach that Josh has a perfectly good youth pastor who has probably shared all sorts of things with him by now. But that didn't seem to satisfy Zach and I figured it really wasn't any of my business anyway.

Furthermore, why should I resent <u>anyone</u> wanting to share Jesus with someone as shallow as Josh? I, of all people, should know how badly he needs it. It's just that I'm trying so hard to keep some space between me and the guy who (not so long ago) caused me so much pain. And, let me say here and now, just because I haven't gone on and on in my diary about Josh Miller and how badly he broke my heart <u>does not mean that I am over him.</u> Ha! If only it were so. The hideous truth is, I am scared to death that if he snapped his fingers at me, I might actually come running back to him.

The worst part is that I'm even more afraid that I might possibly turn my back on God! I just couldn't live with myself if I did that. So, please, is it too much to ask to keep Josh Miller completely out of my life?

GOD, I'M NOT ASKING THAT YOU STRIKE THE GUY DEAD OR ANYTHING THAT DRASTIC, BUT COULDN'T YOU JUST KEEP HIM AWAY FROM ME? I'M SURE NO GOOD CAN COME OF HAVING HIM AROUND. WHAT IF HE AND ZACH SHOULD BECOME FRIENDS? I DON'T KNOW WHAT I'D DO! PLEASE, HELP ME, GOD. AMEN.

April 7, Saturday (strangely answered prayers)

Last week, Zach invited Beanie and me to go to a Christian rock concert. I know that sounds like an oxymoron. (Don't you just love that word? My writing teacher, Miss Tyler, uses it a lot, and it means when words seem to contradict one another—like an "honest politician" or a "tidy pig.") A music group that Zach says is really good was coming to a city that's a couple hours from here, and Zach wanted to drive over and see it. The one good thing about my parents' marital problems (which still remain sadly unresolved although I did give my dad a piece of my mind this week) is that Mom rarely questions where I go, and she seems to trust Beanie a lot more, and she likes Zach too.

So anyway, Beanie comes skipping up to my door around five o'clock as planned (we want to get there in time to eat and make it to the concert in time to get good seats). I climb into Zach's backseat (not because he and Beanie are dating or anything, but because she's known him longer than me and I don't want to intrude), but who do you suppose is sitting in the back of Zach's car? JOSH MILLER!

Now, this is just way too much for me! I'm about ready to scream and bail, but Zach is already taking off down the street. I actually wonder if I could possibly shove Josh out of the moving vehicle without making too much noise. Instead I just glare at him, and then finally, in a really icy voice, I say, "You guys didn't tell me that anyone else was joining us tonight."

Well, Zach just sort of laughs then says, "Sorry, Caitlin, I told Josh that you might not appreciate his company, but he insisted on coming anyway."

I narrow my eyes and then turn to face Josh. "You insisted on coming?" Well, he just sort of shrugs, then smiles that stupid Matt Damon smile that used to just melt me. Not today!

"Yeah," he says somewhat sheepishly. "Zach told me about this rock concert where they sing about Jesus, and it sounded kind of interesting to me. I asked if I could tag along."

Well, I hated to spoil this evening for everyone, but I was really getting upset. So I said, "Fine! But is it really necessary for you to sit next to me?" Then I gave Beanie a hard shove in the front seat (figuring she had as much to do with this as anyone) and said, "If someone doesn't do some seat switching and fast, I may just take a flying leap and jump right out of this vehicle."

Josh laughed and said, "Yeah, I've seen her jumping at the track meets, I'm pretty sure she could do it."

I turned and looked at him (curious but saying nothing and showing no expression). Finally, Zach reached a place where he could safely pull over, and Beanie and Josh changed seats. "Thank you," I said in a stiff voice once we started moving again. Then I gave Beanie a scathing look that I hoped was worth about a million really furious words.

After a few minutes, the three of them began to chat (quite congenially I must admit), and I suddenly felt like the odd man out. That made me really, really mad! I'm thinking how dare Josh come in here and mess up my happy world. I mean, already (because of him) I have been thrown out of his "elite" world, what right does he have to come in here and ruin mine? I'd really been looking forward to this concert!

I tried praying, but all I could think of was, "God, how could you? Especially when I specifically asked you to keep Josh at a distance!" Then, after about an hour of moping, I began to listen to what the three of them were talking about. It turned out Josh was asking Zach some fairly deep questions about faith and stuff. Real thinking kinds of questions. I could tell he was in a similar place to where he'd been on that stupid ski retreat weekend. I began to feel guilty about my attitude.

I've heard that God works in some pretty strange ways, and maybe I just needed to back off a little and allow that God might actually touch Josh's life by using my two dearest friends. Why was I being so selfish anyway? So, I gave the whole thing up to God. If this was meant to be, I sure didn't want to stand in God's way or be a wet blanket. At that point I actually began to warm up a little, entering the conversation here and there. At dinner (where I made sure Beanie sat right next to me) things got even better. But still I tried to avoid all eye contact with Josh. I just wasn't ready for that. When the concert began, I grabbed Beanie and made sure she sat right next to me. I don't think she was too happy about that, because to tell you the truth I think she's starting to think of Zach as more than a friend these days, but I didn't give her a choice.

Somehow, during the intermission, the seating got switched around (and in Josh's defense I think it was Beanie who did the switching) so I just decided to totally ignore Josh and focus all my attention on the band performing on the stage (which as it turned out were pretty good). Finally the concert ended, but the maddening thing was that we got separated on our way out, and naturally I ended up stuck in the crowd with Josh. I don't know exactly why this was so horribly frustrating to me (other than all the previous things I've already mentioned), but for some reason it was so bad that I was actually embarrassingly close to tears. All I could think was, why did this keep happening to me?

It was about at this point when Josh leaned over and said he had something to tell me. I looked up at him in pure frustration and said, "What?" in a rather hostile voice.

Then he calmly said, "You have every right to hate my guts, Caitlin. And it seems pretty apparent that you do. But I just want to tell you I'm sorry about everything that happened on that ski retreat and the whole thing with Jenny afterwards. I know it was wrong of me and I made a great, huge mess of everything. I'm really sorry I hurt you like that. But I'll understand if you don't want to forgive me." Well, I must admit that took me by surprise, and by that time we were almost out to the parking lot, but I figured I better clear this up right then.

"Well, Josh," I said, hoping to sound more gracious than I felt, "I suppose I <u>have</u> to forgive you, because that's what being a Christian is all about, which I am, by the way, and I have absolutely no intention of messing <u>that</u> up. And yes, you did hurt me—you hurt me a lot."

Then something occurs to me, right out of the blue, something I haven't actually seen until just this moment, but I decide to go ahead and say it anyway. "I suppose I should really be thankful, Josh, because due to the fact that you were such a total sleaze, I actually began to look for God in a really serious way. And I found him, and since that moment my life has been going pretty well—other than the fact that you keep showing up, that is!"

Just then I spotted Beanie and Zach and began hurrying toward them. I could hear Josh chuckling as he jogged behind me. "Well, you sure know how to cut a guy down to size," he said just before we reached them. Without answering him, I grabbed Beanie and made certain she sat in the back with me. I didn't care how badly she wanted to sit next to Zach, and I wouldn't mind telling her so later!

That was pretty much that. In some ways I guess I should be thankful for everything that happened this evening, even if it was uncomfortable. Maybe it was just God's way of giving me the opportunity to take care of some unfinished business—closure, you know. Maybe now I can move on in my life whether Josh Miller happens to be lurking about or not. Most of all I hope he's not. Yet to be totally honest, a small part of me hopes that he is (but it's a stupid part of me that I really do hate!).

THIRTEEN

April 8, Sunday (Easter Sunday, and a mishmash of thoughts)

In youth group today, Clay talked about forgiveness again. He told about how when Jesus went to the cross it was the perfect example of forgiveness (being willing to die to yourself to forgive another).

I listened pretty carefully, since that's been the main theme of my life lately. Actually, he talked almost as much about unforgiveness. He said when we refuse to forgive others, it's impossible for us to receive God's forgiveness. That's why Jesus said, "Forgive as I forgave you." Clay said that means to forgive totally (like Jesus did on the cross—nothing halfway about that!). And then he challenged us to search our hearts to see if there was anyone we needed to forgive today.

I have to admit that I haven't totally forgiven my dad for leaving us (not to mention Belinda). To be honest,

I think I haven't totally forgiven Josh either. Although I do think I've forgiven Jenny. I'll have to keep working on Josh and Dad and Belinda. But Clay said that God can help us to forgive, and so I've been asking for help. I guess that's as good a place as any to start.

Clay is so wise and spiritual. I can't believe he's only eighteen. Maybe it's because his mother died when he was little. Anyway, I'm sure he's spent his whole life serving and believing in God (and so he's way ahead of me in that regard). Sometimes it just seems like he has <u>all</u> the answers, and I think I could sit and listen to him for about a year and a half and not get a bit tired of hearing him. Okay, does that mean I have a crush on him? Actually, I'm not entirely sure. I suppose I just might. Still, I'm trying really hard not to think of him like that, because I understand how distracting that can be in a good relationship. Right now I'm just so glad to have him as a good friend. It's true that I really do admire him. And I happen to know he doesn't have a girlfriend (Beanie actually asked him that right in the middle of youth group!).

Speaking of romance, I was totally on the money with Beanie and Zach. She told me today that their relationship has changed recently, and that they are definitely much more than friends now. I acted like I was all happy for her and everything (I mean, she hasn't had a boyfriend since middle school and that was just puppy love anyway), but the truth is, it worries me a little. Mostly I'm afraid that if they run into problems, or break up, they might end up losing what seems to have been a really great friendship. But on the other hand (maybe I'm just being too negative) who knows, they might end up having a really amazing romance! They're both trying really hard to follow God. I'm sure they know what they're doing. And I wouldn't dare say anything negative to Beanie right now (especially considering my level of expertise in such matters), and besides, I just don't want to rain on her parade (which according to Miss Tyler is a tired old cliché and should never be used in good writing).

Now, here's the deal with my dad. Last week I confronted him, and it went surprisingly well. He told me that the only reason he had been with Belinda that night was to end things with her. Well, I ask you, do you take a woman out to dinner to break up? I guess it works in his favor that it wasn't a fancy restaurant (although they do serve pasta dishes at the pizza place). Anyway, I sort of believe him (not totally though).

He and my mom went out again this week. And today I hear that he is wanting to move back in with us (which Mom says probably has as much to do with money as love). My mom's not sure what she wants to do, but Aunt Steph is encouraging her to take him back (something she never would've said just a year ago!). So, my mom told him she's "thinking" about it. Here's what worries me (self-centered as it is): What if my dad moves back in and starts getting all uptight about how much I've been getting to do lately. Like, I can go pretty much where I want with my friends, and mom even lets me drive her car, and all sorts of things. I really don't want to lose all this freedom just because my dad decides to get all paranoid again.

But here's the really hard part, I know the Bible says I'm supposed to obey my parents, so if my dad is all super strict and uptight, does that mean I really have to do what he says? What if I want to challenge him about something that seems totally unfair. Oh, crud!

(something I found in my Bible this evening)

"Don't be anxious about anything, but pray about everything..."

Okay, I guess there's no point in getting all worked up over what my dad may or may not do if he does or does not move back home. I guess I'll just pray about the whole thing, and wait and see what happens.

April 12, Thursday (major confusion)

Okay, here I am having what I think is a pretty good week. Track practice has been going well. No big huge conflicts at school. Miss Tyler even read one of my stories out loud to the class (as an example of "excellent" writing!). And Jenny has actually spoken to me several times (not that I want to get all involved with her again). Plus it looks like my family's getting back together this coming weekend. So for the most part life is basically good.

Then at the end of track practice this afternoon (after a good workout) I'm enjoying a quiet moment in the spring sunshine, relaxing by myself on the big landing pad in the high jump pit. Just minding my own business and watching cloud formations in the sky. And definitely not looking for any company. So, along comes Josh Miller, and he flops down right next to me! I just roll my eyes and ask who invited him over. He laughs (like I'm joking, which I'm actually not!) then starts to talk to me in a real serious voice.

Part of me says, get up and run, Caitlin! But another part is curious and wants to listen. Then Josh tells me that he too has accepted Christ as his personal Savior at his church last week (on Easter Sunday). I smile and say I'm glad for him, and I really am. Then I get up because I want to leave, but he reaches over and grabs my hand. "That's not all," he says looking right at me with those clear blue eyes. "I broke up with Jenny today."

Well, that's fine and dandy, but what does it have to do with me, I wonder. And so, I just say, "Oh..." and stare at him blankly, wishing he wasn't so darned good looking (and now even more so with that golden tan starting to deepen across his face, his arms, his legs). But wait a minute, I'm getting sidetracked here. So he continues, apologizing all over again about all the stuff that happened over a month ago.

I just shrug and say, "I thought we'd taken care of that."

Then he hits me with, "But it seems like you haven't really forgiven me, Caitlin. It's like you're still holding something against me."

"Oh..." I say again. "I guess I'm still working on that. I'm getting lots closer." And then I smile. "And in fact, Josh, I think I <u>have</u> forgiven you—just now."

Well, he's still holding onto my hand, which I must admit is making me pretty nervous. Then he smiles that big Matt Damon smile and it feels like I'm having a major meltdown. Now what do I do? How do I act? What's going on here? And the sun is warm, and the breeze is fresh, and I'm certain I can actually taste the romance drifting over the air. And I'm scared to pieces that he's going to kiss me—and I suppose I'm equally worried that he's not. We just sit there for what feels like an hour, but is actually about a minute.

Then I say, "I'm happy for you, Josh—I mean about accepting Christ. And I guess, if it was the right thing to break up with Jenny, then I'm happy for you about that too."

Then he finally lets go of my hand and says, "I was hoping that we could be friends, Caitlin. I really do like you and I know I blew it the first time with you. I was hoping you'd give me a second chance."

Now, I'm feeling totally confused. Okay, it's fine that he wants to be friends, I guess. But the fact is I'm starting to have all these romantic feelings for him—like crazy! <u>Now</u> he's saying he wants to be friends! Fortunately, common sense kicks in and I quickly agree, saying being friends would be just fine with me, and a couple of other things that I can't even remember right now. But the whole time I'm thinking, what is going on with me?

And now I know I'll have to spend the whole night in prayer just to get over these feelings. Which is what I've been doing, and while it helps a lot, I'm still worried. I don't think I even trust myself anymore. We have a track meet tomorrow (it's at home so there's no need to worry about some long sweaty bus ride), but I wonder how I'll act towards him—or how he'll act towards me.

DEAR GOD, HELP ME. I FEEL LIKE I'M LOST IN THE WILDERNESS TRYING TO FIND MY WAY AND I'M NOT EVEN SURE WHICH WAY TO TURN.

April 13, Friday (mixed feelings)

My Dad came to my track meet today (Mom had to go watch Ben's baseball game). I took first in high jump (no real competition to speak of there) but I didn't even place in long jump (scratched twice and the third jump was really lame). Anyway, when my events were over I went up into the stands to say hi to my dad and sit with him for a while. It was pretty nice of him to leave work early to attend my meet, and I'm trying to be more friendly to him and getting used to the idea that he's coming back into our lives.

Anyway, while I'm sitting up there, Josh comes bouncing up the stairs. I can feel my face growing warm as I realize he's heading right toward us. "Hi," he says as he sits down right beside me. Then I have to introduce him to my dad, calling him "my friend, Josh Miller." They chat briefly and then Josh takes off again.

"Nice kid," says Dad, eyeing me carefully. "Is he really

just a friend?" Now, for some reason, this irritates me more than it probably should.

"What do you mean?" I ask somewhat sharply.

"All I mean, Catie, is that it just seems like he might be more than a friend. I was just curious, is all."

I shrug and shake my head. "He's <u>just</u> a friend, Dad." Then I go back down to the field. But I'm wondering why my dad was so curious about Josh. Is he getting all ready to give me some big speech about how "Christians should act"? I mean, that stuff might be a little hard to stomach, especially coming from a man who only recently nearly nuked his entire marriage. But I decided not to think about that.

Then something pretty strange happened in one of the last sprint races. Josh actually beat Zach by just a hair and took first place in the 100 meters. But the part that is weird is that Josh didn't get all puffed up by winning; instead he turned around and shook Zach's hand and then patted him on the back. It was no help as far as my troubled heart is concerned. (I mean, for the fact that it only served to further endear Josh towards me—something I could really do without right now, thank you very much!)

Then Josh came straight over to me and what could I do other than congratulate him, so I stuck out my hand and he took it, then pulled me into a long hug. Okay, now let me say this: Beanie and I have been hugging Zach each time he wins, and we hug each other too. It's something we've been doing ever since we started going to

youth group. <u>Everyone</u> hugs there—even the crosstown
rivals. It's like brotherly love, you know. But I had
absolutely no intention of hugging Josh, especially in front
of everyone (including Jenny who I happen to know was
there—and I'm sure was none too happy considering Josh
just broke up with her yesterday). I know it's stupid, but
I'm sure my face was flaming red when I finally stepped
away from him. But then he looked down into my eyes
and said, "For some reason, I think God helped me with
this race today. But Zach will probably take all the
rest." Then he laughed.

Now what healthy, red-blooded American girl wouldn't
melt down just a little at a scene like that? And did I
mention he looks just like Matt Damon (same sparkling blue
eyes, mussed-up blond hair, big white-toothed smile)? So,
what can I say? That Caitlin Renee O'Conner is human?
Big duh! It's true, my heart did beat a little faster and
for a moment (okay, <u>more</u> than a moment!), I wished we
were more than friends. But honestly, deep down, I'm glad
that it's nothing more. I'm not ready. I don't even think
Josh is ready. Maybe in time...

After the track meet, I rode home with my dad. Of
course, he mentioned the embrace with Josh down on the
track, but I quickly set him straight, saying we always
hugged to congratulate each other—hadn't he been
watching? That seemed to shut him up. After we got
home, we waited for Mom and Benjamin, and then we all
went out for Chinese food. We actually had a pretty
decent time. Tomorrow my dad is moving back home. And

my mom seems okay about it. They plan to go out tomorrow night to celebrate. I just hope he's really over Belinda now. I'm not sure that my mom could go through this whole thing again and still take him back.

April 15, Sunday (dating decisions)

Dad didn't understand why we didn't want to go back to our old church with him, but none of us really did. Mom told him he was free to go wherever he pleased, but that we were going to Faith Fellowship. And so he decided to join us. Afterwards he complained about a few things (like why didn't they have their own church building and how the sound system sucked), but other than that, he seemed to sort of like it. He even said the pastor, although young, was pretty good.

Today in youth group, Clay invited us to just ask questions and talk about whatever we liked. It was pretty fun. But what I really wanted to ask about was the whole girl-guy relationship stuff, and how we're supposed to handle this as Christians. And just as I was thinking about how best to say it (remember how I write better than I speak?), a sophomore girl from McFadden (Beth Alberts) asked it for me. First, Clay said, there were some general guidelines in the Bible, mostly like not having sex outside of marriage, and then he said that beyond that he thought it was something everyone had to figure out for themselves—like a personal conviction (which he has told us about before).

Then he went on to say, "I know that for me, it would

be wrong to get romantically involved with a girl right
now." (And I think I saw a curtain of disappointment fall
over Beth's face just then, but it could just be my imagination.) Then he asked others what they thought about
girl-guy relationships. Several people said a few different
things—more questions than anything. And I was pretty
curious if Zach or Beanie would speak up, then Zach did.

He said, "Clay's right about it being a personal conviction. I think some people can handle having a boy-girl relationship if they keep their priorities straight, but it can be
harmful to others."

Beanie nodded then added, "Like Zach and I are
really good friends, and we have been for several
months, but if our relationship slowly grows into something
more and we feel in our hearts that we're obeying God,
then it's okay."

I glanced over at Clay, curious as to his thoughts, and
I suspect he wasn't totally convinced, but he didn't say
anything. We all kicked the subject around for the rest
of our time, not really coming to any clear-cut conclusions
other than sex outside of marriage was a big no-no.
Although a couple kids even questioned this, but Clay
very gently offered to talk to them privately about it
later, which I think was nice, but Clay's just like that.

Tonight, I'm thinking about all this stuff too. Okay, I'll
admit it, I'm thinking about Josh as well. I know he said
we're just going to be friends, but it wouldn't surprise me
if he asks me out someday. And I want to get this whole
thing straightened out in my mind just in case he does.

And if he doesn't—well, it wouldn't hurt for me to think about this anyway.

So, I'm wondering, what's wrong with dating? To tell the truth, I think it might be a good thing. I mean, it teaches us how to act around the opposite sex, right? What's wrong with that? It's not like dating is going to lead everyone right into having sex (like my dad used to imply), which, by the way, brings me to a very interesting point. If dating leads to sex, then how can my dad claim that he escaped without having <u>it</u> when he was obviously seeing (shall we say dating?) Belinda all that time? I'll have to remember that point if Dad ever tries to discourage me from dating in the future. Okay, so for now, I think dating is okay, but sex isn't. That seems simple and clear-cut enough.

FOURTEEN

April 20, Friday (on being friends)

Rumors have been circulating this week that I'm after Josh Miller. The whole thing makes me really mad, considering how hard I've tried to stay out of the whole thing with him (ever since my big heartbreak that is). And I don't think I've actually done a single thing that could've been misconstrued as "being after" him or anyone else for that matter. I mean, we talk occasionally at track practice, but he's ALWAYS the one who initiates it—just ask anyone on the team.

Beanie said she heard Heather and Jenny talking in her math class today and she figures that's where the rumors started. It turns out Jenny is just furious because she wanted to go to the prom with Josh. I'm thinking, now, is going to the prom with a certain person so important that you'd stay together no matter what, just so you could attend some silly dance with him? Of course, then I have to admit I did the same thing with the Valentine Dance. Now I know how stupid I was then. Apparently Jenny still thinks like that. But if you ask me, it's completely shallow and totally dumb! I mean, Jenny could get any guy to take her to the prom. Why doesn't she hit on Nathan Parker again? I heard he's not dating anyone right now.

Anyway, all week long I've been telling myself not to get all worked up about these stupid rumors. That's all they are. And anyone who knows me knows that I'm not chasing after Josh. (Okay, so they don't know what I'm thinking—even I don't always know that—but even if I'm thinking about him occasionally, I'm not showing anything on the outside!)

I guess I shouldn't have been too shocked when on the way home from our track meet (an away one) Josh sits by me and asks if I've heard the rumor. I say yes and try to laugh it off as a big joke. Then he gets sort of serious and says, "Well, it wouldn't be impossible—things like that do happen."

I turn and look at him (big mistake!) and then quickly say, "Sure, things like that happen. But we're just friends, right?"

He nods sort of slowly then adds, "Is it okay for friends to go out together?"

Now, I wasn't really sure what he meant by that. "You mean like going out to get a Coke or something?" I ask, feeling pretty dense.

Then he smiles. "Yeah, Caitlin, you know how friends do."

So, I say, "Sure, I don't see why not," but I can feel my cheeks starting to grow warm because I was thinking he'd been going to ask me out on a date—and I know I would've said yes.

But he didn't and I guess I had sort of mixed feelings about it.

After we got back to school and showered and dressed, Beanie and I were waiting for Zach (to give us a ride) and he came out with Josh (in fact, they're getting to be fairly good friends). Then Zach says, "Hey, do you girls want to come with us and get some pizza or something?" Beanie looks at me questioningly (remembering, I'm sure, how I wanted to kill her the last time they tried to set up what felt like a double date) so I quickly said, "Yeah, sure. I'm starved."

Josh let me use his cell phone to call home (since my dad's back I'm trying to check in a little better), and, of course, Beanie and Zach didn't need to check in with anyone, then we took off in Josh's Jeep Wrangler (with me in the front and Beanie and Zach in the back). This time I didn't even complain! So we went out for pizza and then we played some silly video games at this hokey arcade that Benjamin likes to go to sometimes. And that was it. I'm still not sure if that even qualifies as a date— or was it just friends doing something together? The latter, I think.

Anyway, it didn't seem to be such a problem. Although I must admit to being slightly uncomfortable when I realized that Beanie and Zach were actually kissing in the backseat. For some reason that bothered me. I'm not even sure why.

April 21, Saturday (a date)

Josh called me at home today. He asked me if I wanted to go see a movie with him—a new release that I'd actually been wanting to see. I was tempted to ask him if this was a date or just friends doing something together. But decided not to. In my mind I was thinking it was a date. And that was okay.

As it turned out, my dad jumped to the same conclusion when I announced that I was going to a movie with Josh. I looked him right in the eye, all ready to proceed with my Belinda Defense, but he didn't say anything. I could tell he wanted to. But Mom was right there too, and I don't think he wanted to make a scene. Very wise, Dad. Anyway, it took about twelve outfits before I could decide what to wear. It's getting pretty warm now and I finally decided on a blouse that's cut sort of short around my midriff, and I suppose a little skin was showing. But it's no big deal. At least not to me. However, I'm pretty certain I saw my dad's nostrils flair as I went out the door with Josh. Get over it, Dad.

The movie was pretty good. I honestly think they could have handled the sex scene differently. I mean did the camera have to go in so close that you could almost smell their breath when they were kissing? If my dad was worried about me showing a little skin, then he should see <u>this</u>. I'll admit it, it was a little embarrassing! And, yes, it was rated R. But why do they make movies that they know kids will want to see and then rate them

R—isn't it just to make us feel grown-up and want to go? I
don't get it. They never even check for ID at the ticket
booth.

But here's the truth, and I would never in a million
years admit this to my dad (or any other grown-up for
that matter), but seeing these people up there practically doing EVERYTHING on the big screen somehow makes
it seem like it might actually be okay to do it.

Now, I know that it's wrong—and I know what I've
said—but somehow seeing it like that sort of makes it
seem acceptable (and the characters in the movie
weren't even married!). And while I'm on this subject, have
you ever noticed how almost all the TV shows and com-
mercials and everything else just seem to say <u>it's</u> okay? I
mean, why is that? If it's not okay, then why doesn't someone make them stop sending these messages? That's
what they are—messages. And we all know what the
messages say, don't we?

Okay, you've probably already guessed where I'm
going with this. And my promise from the start of this
diary has been to be <u>totally</u> honest. Well, after the movie
we got some ice cream and then we went for a walk in
the park. Sounds pretty innocent, doesn't it? Well, one
thing led to another and pretty soon we were kissing. I
won't go into all the details, except to say that it felt
good. Really good! And Josh's hands were on me—kind of
like in the movie—and although it made me nervous, it
felt good too. But suddenly we were both breathing
really hard and pressed up against each other and I

knew that something was going wrong here. And I knew it was up to me to break it up.

So I gave him a big push away from me, caught my breath, and told him we had to stop. It took him a moment, but then he finally said, "Yeah, I got carried away. I'm sorry, Caitlin." And well, what could I say? I mean, it was as much my fault as his, wasn't it? So I suggested we call it a night and he drove me home without saying much.

He walked me to my front door and apologized again. "I want it to be different with us, Caitlin," he said. "I want to do things right <u>with you</u>." Well, I knew he was referring to how things had been with Jenny, and I must admit although I was relieved that he wanted to "do things right" the idea of him and Jenny together (doing <u>it</u>) made me extremely uncomfortable. I know I said something in response, but I can't recall exactly what except that it was pretty insignificant. Then he kissed me good night.

And now I'm in here wrestling with all these confusing feelings. I really want to talk to someone about it, but don't know who. Not my mom, and for sure not my dad. I know what Aunt Steph would say now (I wonder what she would've said last year!). I cannot imagine talking to Clay about anything like this—sometimes I wish Josh was more like Clay (or do I?). Maybe Beanie can help me. I'm sure she'll understand all this. In fact, she's probably going through a lot of the very same things. Unless what those two suggested in youth group is really true, and that they really do have everything under control. But how could they possibly? I've seen them making out! Anyway, I'll ask Beanie to do something with me after church tomorrow, maybe go to the mall or something, and then we'll talk.

April 22, Sunday (confusing things)

Beanie's not much help. She still maintains that she and Zach are handling everything just fine—but at the same time I almost get the impression there's something more going on. And she says that they even talk about _it_, and actually discuss why or why not they should or shouldn't. Now, I'm sorry, but that creeps me out. I cannot imagine talking to Josh about something like that! I mean, they never talk about it in the movies; one thing just leads to another and the next thing you know they're doing it— right in your face! Okay, so they're acting. But you know what I mean!

Anyway, I warned Beanie that she better be careful. Just because we're Christians doesn't mean that we can't get hurt. I mean, like last week, I observed Jenny a few times (when she didn't know I was looking) and she just looked so sad and I wondered how she must feel after having done _it_ with Josh (yes, and it still makes me mad!) but does she feel used now? I remember how I felt after just making out with him for one weekend and getting dumped. I felt worse than really bad dog crap. I can't imagine how she must feel now. I don't want anything like that to happen to Beanie—or Zach either for that matter. Or me.

April 25, Wednesday (new developments)

So far this week has been okay for the most part, considering. The only snag being that Jenny heard that Josh and I went out on Saturday (probably due to Hilary Weiss—she saw us at the theater and has a very big mouth!). And I may be slightly paranoid, but I thought I saw Jenny looking at me like she'd like to have me murdered or something. Josh has been joining Zach and Beanie and me and a few other kids (from track and the youth group or whatever) at lunch—almost like we have our own little clique now (not that I'm into that stuff anymore!). But it's nice to have friends. Anyway, Josh says not to worry about Jenny, that he's handled everything with her and she needs to just get over it. Truthfully I've never considered her to be a vengeful person. I guess I just wish she didn't hate me. Maybe in time...

It's Josh's birthday this weekend and he invited me to do something with him on Saturday, I'm not sure what, but I said yes. Now I wonder if that means I should get him a present—and I want to, but I'm just not sure what it should be. I mean, I want it to be something nice, but I don't want it to look like I'm real serious or anything. Hopefully I'll think of something by Saturday.

For the first two days of this week, Josh only kissed me a couple of times (mostly after he dropped me off after track practice—and I'm afraid my dad was watching yesterday). But today, I was lying in the high

jump pit again after practice relaxing and getting some
rays and Josh joined me, and the next thing I knew we
were really kissing big time. Is it something in the air? But
I've noticed a lot of kids are getting into this whole spring
romance thing. Maybe it's always been there but I'm just
noticing it more now. (Like if you get this really cool pink
sweater and suddenly it seems like the whole world is
wearing pink sweaters!) I think it has something to do with
spring. Anyway, there we were getting all hot and passion-
ate right there in the high jump pit, and that's when
Coach Reynolds walks up and says, "You two done practicing for the day?" Well, man, you should've seen me leap—
talk about a high jump!

But Josh just sort of sits up real nonchalant and says,
"Practicing, Coach? I thought this was the real thing."
Well, Coach didn't laugh, but he did look at me curiously,
almost as if he wanted to say something. Then he shook
his head and walked away. I felt so stupid—and kind of
slutty too. I told Josh I'd see him later then jogged back
to the locker room by myself. Why is becoming an adult so
difficult?

Sometimes I remember how simple my life used to be
when I was still a little girl. I mean, it was so nice not
being all concerned about things like boys and sex and
all that kind of stuff. Sometimes I wonder, why does all
that have to change anyway? I mean, why do we have to
grow up? It's one of those things I want God to explain to
me someday. It's not like I don't enjoy the things that
come with growing up—good grief, the problem seems to be

that I enjoy them <u>too</u> much (or at least I'm afraid I do).
So, I guess my other question is this: If these things are so
enjoyable, why do they have to be wrong? Okay, I think
that's enough questions for the night.

April 27, Friday (two warnings)

Kind of a strange day today. I mean, the track meet
went okay, and everything between me and Josh seems
to be okay (and under control). But earlier today, just
after lunch, after Josh told me good-bye (and, yes, gave
me a quick kiss) Jenny came up to me. She's all by herself
(not that normal) and has this sort of blank expression on
her face (not angry or hurt—just blasé) and she looks me
in the eye and says, "Be careful, Caitlin." Then she walks
away. That's it. End of story. Now, I didn't tell anyone
else about this, because I really don't know what to
make of it. Was she threatening me? Was she warning me
that she's going to get Josh back? Or what? Finally, I
decided it just wasn't worth worrying about. But it's still
bugging me a little. I've even considered calling her to
find out what she meant.

Josh dropped me at home after the meet (which we
won by the way) and then had to hurry to meet his parents for dinner at a fancy restaurant (for his birthday—
he and I will celebrate tomorrow, which gave me time to
get him a present at the mall tonight). He kissed me and
then promised to call later.

Well, as fate would have it, my dad was just getting
home (I hadn't noticed) and watched the whole thing,

and was waiting for me on the porch. "Looks like you and Josh have become more than friends," he began. I just shrugged and said, "Things can change."

Then Dad set down his briefcase and put a hand on my shoulder (I'm sure he thought it was a nice fatherly gesture, but I felt pretty sure I knew what was coming, so I probably acted kind of stiff). Anyway he told me that he hoped that the mistakes he'd made with Belinda wouldn't make it so that I never wanted to listen to his advice anymore. I thought, when did I ever want to listen to his advice before? at least about boys and sex; but I didn't say this. Then he said that he loved me and didn't want to see me get hurt and that he didn't want to say too much, but that he wanted me to be careful. That got my attention because it's what Jenny had said to me.

"Careful about what?" I asked with suspicion.

He looked kind of blank, like he hadn't really expected me to respond, then said, "You know, just take care and don't try to grow up too fast. Don't let anyone push you into anything you're not ready for."

I nodded. "Okay. I don't usually let anyone push me into anything." Then I smiled. "But thanks for the advice, I guess."

So, that was two people telling me to be careful. Probably just a coincidence, but kind of funny just the same. Anyway, I went to the mall with Beanie and Zach, and Zach finally talked me into getting Josh a Bible (leather with his name on it—took a whole month's allowance too). But I think maybe Zach's right (and obviously he knows what a guy would like). Anyway, I think it's a pretty good gift. It says that I really care about Josh in a spiritual way and as a good friend. And for now, I think that's enough.

FIFTEEN

April 28, Saturday (the birthday date)

Okay, if I were to describe the perfect date—tonight would have definitely been it. Well, almost anyway (but I'll get to that part later). Josh had called last night to let me know we would be going out to dinner at a special place and to dress up. I borrowed this really cool light blue top from Aunt Steph (I'd seen her wear it to church once and I knew it must've cost a fortune)—I also knew it would go perfectly with my favorite long skirt (which it did by the way). Then I wore the silver and quartz necklace and earring set that Mom got me for Christmas.

I think I looked pretty good. And Josh thought so too. He always says that I look just like Gwyneth Paltrow (and even though Aunt Steph says the same thing, I don't really think so), but anyway, I know I looked okay. It turned out he was taking us (actually his parents paid for the whole thing) to this restaurant that's on a boat

out on the lake just outside of town, and they have
these little row boats to take you out to the big boat.
And it was all just so magical and wonderful—with little
white lights all reflecting all over the water and all
these waiters and people treating us just like we're grown-
ups. It was just so totally cool. And the dinner was
absolutely delicious—for the first time in my life I had
real lobster, with a shell and everything! (Josh said I
could order anything I wanted.)

Then we had our dessert (cherry-chocolate torte)
out on the deck with these little torches burning all
around. And then Josh asked me if I'd go to the prom with
him!!! Of course I said yes! Honestly, I wondered if heaven
could be any better than this! After we finished eating
we lingered on the deck for a while. It was one of those
warm spring nights where you can almost feel summer in
the air. We just stood there and looked out on the city
lights and stuff—and, okay, <u>kissing</u>. But, how, pray tell,
could I not indulge in a little kissing under <u>those</u> circumstances. It was like being in a movie or something and so
incredibly romantic!

By the way, Josh really liked his birthday gift too. He
said the only Bible he owned was from childhood and
looked pretty juvenile, and that this one really meant a
lot to him.

So anyway, we finally thought it was time to leave.
But we didn't really know what to do because it seemed
too early to call it a night, but too late to catch a movie
or anything else. So, Josh drove up to a spot that overlooks

the town (yes, it's the place where kids go to make out—but also to enjoy the view, which was what I was sure we were going to do). As you can guess, one thing led to another and before I knew what had hit me, we had progressed further than before and it was really difficult to put on the brakes (for me too!). Just the same I made it perfectly clear that we HAD to stop right then and there. And then we got into this little fight. Nothing really huge, but it kind of spoiled what would have otherwise been a perfect evening. And it did hurt my feelings a little that Josh insinuated that I had worn a really sensuous outfit just to torment and tease him—which I did not, by the way! I only dressed up because he'd said to; I didn't even think it was a "sensuous" outfit in the first place, but I'm starting to realize that guys and girls definitely think differently about a few things!

Josh drove me home (in silence), but by the time we reached my house, he apologized to me. I apologized too, thinking I should've seen this whole thing coming and stopped things sooner than I did. I know Josh was pretty frustrated, but I couldn't think of anything else to say that would make anything better. So I just thanked him for a really great evening and said good night—without even one last good night kiss. I felt kind of bad about <u>that</u> once I got into the house, but on the other hand, I think we'd done enough kissing tonight to last us both for quite a while!

It wasn't all that late, so I called Beanie up and told her everything (well, not the last part about the fight) but about the dinner, the gift, going to the prom, and all that. And she didn't seem all that excited. In fact, she almost sounded jealous or something. So, I asked her how things were going with her and Zach, and it seems they'd gotten into some big fight (I'm wondering, is it something in the air?). Anyway, I nicely asked her what they had fought about, but she didn't want to tell me. And finally, after a lot of gentle coaxing, she said it was about <u>sex</u>.

Well, I tried not to act all surprised, but simply said, "So, you guys have done it then?"

And she said <u>yes</u>. And for some reason I was totally stunned. But I didn't let on (this is a game I learned how to play while hanging with Jenny). Anyway, Beanie explained that ever since they had done <u>it</u>, they hardly ever talk anymore, and it's like it's all they want to do when they get together, but once they do <u>it</u>, there doesn't seem to be anything left to say or do. So their relationship is suffering. I felt really bad for her, but didn't know what to say.

So I told her I'd pray for them, which she actually seemed to appreciate. That's exactly what I plan to do as soon as I close this book. What I didn't mention to Beanie is that I'll be praying for me and Josh too, and that we don't fall into that same trap. And I must admit after our little fight tonight, I'm feeling pretty worried because it feels like something's lurking around the next corner—just like a hungry wolf that's waiting to devour us and destroy everything. Somehow I just have that awful feeling. And I'm afraid that I won't be able to fight it off.

DEAR GOD, HELP US—HELP US ALL (BEANIE, ZACH, JOSH, ME), HELP US TO KNOW WHAT YOUR WILL IS WITH THESE RELATIONSHIPS. I FEEL SO CONFUSED, AND I THINK I MAY HAVE CHOSEN TO DISOBEY YOU AND THAT WORRIES ME A LOT. I DON'T WANT THAT. I WANT TO LIVE MY LIFE THE WAY YOU WANT ME TO. I KNOW THAT WITHOUT YOU I CAN MAKE A REALLY BIG MESS OF THINGS AND I DON'T WANT THAT. HELP US ALL TO KNOW HOW YOU WANT US TO LIVE. AND HELP US TO LISTEN TO YOU AND TO OBEY. THANK YOU.

May 4, Friday (a very bad night)

This had been a fairly quiet week—up until today that is. To start with, Josh had been sick for the first couple days (he called me on Monday but didn't seem too talkative) which was kind of good, because that little space from him gave me time to think about some things that Clay said at youth group on Sunday. He said that he'd been feeling concerned for some of us (didn't say who) but that he felt we were in some sort of "spiritual danger" (those were his exact words!) and that he'd been praying for us a lot.

After hearing that I've been reading my Bible and praying a lot more. And I've been basically trying to figure everything out. I don't know that I've made much progress, but a couple of things seem clear to me. First of all, Josh and I need to slow things way down in our relationship. More importantly, <u>I need to love God more than I</u>

love Josh. It's something Clay talked about—how the most important thing we can do is to love God (and others too), but we need to love God more than anything (more than our family or friends or even our own lives!). Now, loving God may sound simple enough, but it's not that easy to love him above all else (and like Clay says, God knows our hearts and whether we're being honest or not). And it can be especially difficult when you're sixteen and have a really handsome boyfriend who you really do love a lot! So I'm working on it.

Josh showed back up at school on Wednesday and he seemed quieter too. Which was kind of a relief. And I thought maybe he's been giving these same things some thought too, and I was hoping maybe I could tell him about it, but I haven't really had the right opportunity. Then we had our track meet yesterday and Josh didn't do too well in his events (I didn't do too well either). In fact, none of us did that great and we ended up losing the meet (against a team that wasn't supposed to be that good). I figure you win a few and lose a few. Afterwards, Coach Reynolds gave us this little speech about how these were just earthly races and what really mattered was how we all ran the race of life. Sort of like a little sermon, you know, and to tell the truth, I think we all kind of appreciated it.

Then today, Josh asks me if I'll go with him to his cousin's birthday party tonight (he's a senior at McFadden) and I say, "Sure." So he picks me up around seven and we go on over to the other side of town where, as it turns out, this totally out of control party is raging with absolutely no parents anywhere in sight. And not only is there alcohol flowing like a river, but drugs too. Mostly pot. But before the night is over I notice a couple of other things that make me pretty suspicious and nervous. As soon as I realize what's going on here, I tell Josh I want to go home. But, to my surprise, he's already letting his cousin pour him a drink, and hands me one too.

I'm so stunned that I stupidly take the drink and just stare at him, then I repeat (loudly, to be heard over the music) that I want to go home. He says "in a little," and that he doesn't want to be rude to his cousin on his birthday. Then he assures me he had no idea it was this kind of party. Okay, I guess I believe him and will try to be patient, but the whole thing is creeping me out and I really want to leave. Of course, the only alternative to waiting for Josh would be for me to call home for a ride, which would mean my dad would have to come, since Mom and Aunt Steph went to a baby shower tonight. And if Dad came to get me that would mean a great big lecture and who knows what else. So despite a strong inner nagging to get out of there, I decide to just hang loose. Big mistake, Caitlin.

So, first of all, I dump the drink Josh gave me (I know it's wrong to drink, and I don't want any part of it), then I look for a place to wait it out while Josh "celebrates" with his cousin. Then who should I see here but Andrea LeMarsh (a quiet girl from our Faith Fellowship youth group). First I think I'll try to avoid her, but then I think why? I go right over to her (she's drinking a beer!) and I ask her how she's doing. Well, she practically chokes and I can see that I've really taken her by surprise, but she immediately comes back with what am I doing here, and I explain all about Josh and his cousin and how I didn't know this was a drinking party. Then I look at the beer in her hand and ask if she does this on a regular basis (I guess being ticked at Josh has emboldened me a little). She's getting real embarrassed now and says no, but she just wanted to give it a try. I ask her if she's driving and she says no, she came with friends. I ask if the driver is drinking. She shrugs then asks me the same thing. I tell her he's only having a social drink, which makes her laugh, and that makes me mad.

I tell her to be careful, then I go off to find a quiet place to wait for Josh (Josh's aunt and uncle are obviously rich—their house is enormous!). It seems like kids are everywhere (mostly making out and other things and I'm getting more than a little disgusted and I'm actually considering calling my dad). I finally find an office (unoccupied) and sit down on a leather sofa to wait, deciding that if Josh isn't ready to leave by nine, then I'll call home (and maybe by then my mom will be back).

Just before nine I hear Josh calling my name, and I yell to him that "I'm in here" and he comes in to join me, acting all sorry that he brought me to such a crappy party (but I can smell booze on his breath and by the way he's now slurring his words, I'm pretty sure Andrea was right to laugh!). And then he starts trying to kiss me and getting all mushy and putting his hands all over me, and I shove him away which he actually seems to like. So he starts kind of laughing, and then we have this little wrestling match on the couch (and I'm thinking, <u>who is this guy?</u>). I consider yelling for help, but I think that's kind of silly because this is only Josh for Pete's sake. But at the same time, I'm feeling scared and I'm tired of pushing him off. Then suddenly he gets pretty aggressive and I start to really freak out! And I'm actually afraid that he's going to hurt me! And I do scream!

But we're in a room in the back of the house and the music is so loud that I'm sure no one can hear me. Then suddenly we hear other people yelling and stampeding through the house—and we quickly realize that the cops are here and the party's being busted. Now, I'm not sure which I'm more afraid of—getting arrested and having to call my parents, or Josh. But before I can think Josh grabs me by the arm (and since he knows his way around the house), makes a quick escape through a side door, down the driveway, and into his Jeep which is parked down the street. Then he starts the engine and quietly slips down an alley. I'm shaking so hard, I cannot speak. At any minute I expect to see the flashing blue lights—and I halfway hope that I do.

Finally it's apparent that he's managed to get away, and now I am really, really mad! And I ask him to let me out on the next corner (there's a convenience store right there). Well, of course, he is all over himself saying, "I'm sorry, I got carried away, I didn't mean anything..." He goes on and on, saying he doesn't know what came over him, that he never should've had a drink, how he totally hates himself for doing that, and all sorts of pitiful things. And now I'm actually feeling sorry for him. So I tell him, the only way I'm not getting out of this Jeep right now is if he hands over the keys and I drive the rest of the way. He agrees and I drive straight home.

Out of concern for his safety, I did consider dropping him off at his house first, but I was worried he might not agree to let me take his Jeep after that. And after all I've been through tonight, all I want is to get home safely. Once I'm home (still shaking) I pray that God will safely get him home too. And then I collapse on my bed in tears.

WHAT A TOTAL MESS I AM MAKING OF MY LIFE, GOD. I DON'T KNOW HOW YOU COULD POSSIBLY LOVE SOMEONE AS HOPELESS AND STUPID AS ME. WILL I EVER LEARN HOW TO MAKE GOOD DECISIONS? I KNEW I SHOULD'VE CALLED MY PARENTS THE VERY FIRST THING, BUT I DIDN'T. I'M SO SORRY, GOD; PLEASE, PLEASE FORGIVE ME!

Then like someone pouring a bucket of ice cold water over my head, it occurs to me that I placed myself in a seriously dangerous position tonight.

1) I could have been involved in a drunken driving car accident, or 2) I could have been arrested (really the least of these possibilities), or 3) I could have experienced date rape.

And this is not to mention the serious trouble I could have gotten into with my parents (if they'd known). I could have been grounded for life—which honestly doesn't seem like such a bad idea just now.

But the really weird thing is I don't feel much pleasure in realizing how lucky I was to escape these very near catastrophes. Mostly I feel a deep regret that I am so stupid as to get involved in something like this to begin with.

Okay, you may be thinking that I didn't <u>intentionally</u> do something wrong—like I didn't know it was going to be a drinking party. But let me be totally honest here. I had this gut feeling (call it a still, small voice if you want) but I had a feeling that I was flirting with disaster, dabbling in sin—whatever, but something inside me was sending out warnings.

And, come to think of it, so did Jenny of all people (she told me to be careful). And so did Dad for that matter. Even Clay seemed pretty concerned about us kids in youth group last week. It's like the writing was all over the wall (sorry, Miss Tyler).

Well, here and now I am deciding that something's got to change in me. I will not keep living like this. I know that might mean I have to rethink things with Josh. But after tonight, I'm ready to do that.

Okay, I'll admit I still have strong feelings for him. But I'm not going to be stupid about it. I know that something's wrong with our relationship. I just hope I have the strength to do what's right. Hopefully, I'll actually know what's right when the time comes. And I'll keep praying that God will show me. I'm sure that he will.

But right now, I'm exhausted. All I want to do is sleep—and to thank God for protecting me tonight.

THANK YOU, GOD. I CAN SEE I'VE BEEN A FOOL, AND I'M REALLY SORRY. I'M NOT EVEN TOTALLY SURE WHAT THE NEXT STEP IS FOR ME, BUT I PRAY THAT YOU WILL SHOW ME. I PRAY THAT I WON'T QUESTION YOU, AND THAT I WILL OBEY. THANK YOU AGAIN FOR TAKING CARE OF ME. AND ONCE AGAIN I'M REALLY, REALLY SORRY. AMEN.

SIXTEEN

May 6, Sunday (a ray of hope)

I stayed home all day yesterday. I think I was sort of in shock or something. But anyway, in the afternoon up comes this florist van, and the guy is delivering a bunch of red roses to ME. And they are from Josh, with a handwritten apology. My parents are pretty surprised (of course, I don't show them the note). They want to know what the special occasion is. I just shrug and say I don't know. Then my dad says did I know that red roses are the symbol of true love? I just laugh and say, "Did it occur to you that Josh might just like the color red?" I wonder if I should call him up and say thanks, but somehow I don't want to. In fact, for the first time in weeks I had no desire to see him at all. I wonder how long that will last.

I went to church and youth group today. Surprisingly enough Andrea was there too. We both just sort of looked at each other without saying anything. But I was really curious if she'd been among the kids that got MIPs (minors

in possession), but I didn't ask. Today, Clay brought his gui-
tar and played a song that he wrote. It was so good, I
think he could probably sell it to a recording studio. I
kept looking at him and thinking, why can't Josh be more
like him? Then I started wondering what I'd ever seen in
Josh in the first place. And then I even wondered
(although I felt guilty about this one, but it's the truth) if
Clay ever decided to have a girlfriend, would he consider someone like me? And I instantly thought, no way—
I'd never be good enough for someone like him. And that
made me so sad I almost started to cry. But somehow I
managed to cover it up.

Honestly, I'm wondering if I might be turning into some
sort of basket case. But then, I'm not the only one. Zach
and Beanie seemed out of sorts today too. I remembered
the problems they were having. And suddenly I thought,
man, we are really one screwed up bunch of kids. I wondered if poor Clay has any idea what a mess we are!
But we ended in prayer and Clay said that God had
shown him that we were "all going to do great and power-
ful things—individually and corporately" (those were his
exact words).

Well, at least that was encouraging. If anyone can
make something of a bunch of messed up kids, I'm sure
God can. But now I'm wondering what in the world I'm supposed to do about Josh. To tell the truth (and this is
embarrassing because I used to think Jenny was being
stupid) but I don't want to break up with Josh before I get
a chance to go to the prom with him (and that's not until

the end of May). And anyway, aren't we supposed to forgive one another?

May 9, Wednesday (old habits die hard)

The week started out okay. I think last weekend
knocked some sense into Josh and for the first couple
days he was really polite and not pushy or anything. But
then today (after track practice) I started seeing some
of that old stuff emerging. And I got concerned again. I
mean, all he did was kiss me (a little too long), but it was
enough to send up a danger signal. When I pushed him
away, he got irritated. But I didn't really care at the
time. Although now I'm not so sure.

Everyone at school is talking about the prom, and suddenly everyone seems to be switching boyfriends. Now,
Heather Larson is going with Nathan. And Jenny (rumored
to have broken up Heather and Brian) is going with Brian.
Even Zach and Beanie are planning on going. And I really
want to go.

Quite honestly, something inside me is saying no. Do you
think it could be God? I can't understand why he wouldn't
want me to go and just have a good time (I mean without
doing anything wrong). It seems like that would be a sort of
"victorious" thing to do, wouldn't it? But I'm just not sure.
And since I've been praying that I'd learn to recognize and
obey God's voice, I'm worried that I might actually be
hearing it and yet I'm unwilling to do what he says (especially in this one particular area). I ask you, would a kind
and loving God ask a sixteen-year-old girl to give up a

chance to go to the prom with one of the most popular boys in school (a boy who only recently gave his heart to Jesus)? I just don't think so. But then again, I'm not sure either.

OH, GOD, HELP ME TO FIGURE THIS ALL OUT. AND HELP ME TO BE TRUE TO YOU. I LOVE YOU, GOD. I WANT TO CHOOSE YOU ABOVE ALL ELSE. BUT I MIGHT NEED SOME HELP. AMEN.

May 11, Friday at noon (a very black Friday)

This is the saddest day of my life. I am literally numb with grief.

This morning we heard there had been another school shooting. Only this time it was much, much closer to home. At 8:16 A.M., a freshman boy entered McFadden High and shot about a dozen kids in the cafeteria before a couple of football players jumped him from behind and knocked the automatic weapon from his hands.

Clay Berringer was among those shot. Clay was pronounced dead at 11:20 this morning.

They sent us home from school. They canceled the track meet (not that I would have gone anyway). And now a bunch of people are meeting (from our church) to pray for the rest of the day. I couldn't go. Not yet.

I am so totally devastated I cannot even hold my pen to write legibly. I cannot think. I cannot even pray. I am certain that I will never laugh again. And I am so angry at God for allowing this to happen. Where were the angels that were supposed to protect Clay? How could God take him away from us?

Oh, Clay, dearest, Clay. You were so good, so true, so honest, so very dear. So incredibly good. Oh, Clay, how could God allow you to leave this world when we need you so badly right now? I will never in a hundred years understand this.

My heart is shattered into millions of tiny pieces, and I don't know if I can ever trust God again.

SEVENTEEN

May 11, Friday (later that night)

I finally went to join the members of our church who had gathered to pray for Tony Berringer (Clay's brother and our pastor) as well as the other kids who were shot and their families. Two other kids have died (a senior girl who had almost a four-point GPA, and a junior boy who'd been on the track team and had raced against Zach and Josh). It all seems so unbelievably unfair. The other wounded kids are in varying conditions, but they say most are out of critical danger by now. I just don't get it. Kids killing other kids. Why?

Tony joined us at the prayer meeting this evening. He was being amazingly brave and gracious and even said we must also pray for the shooter (and to forgive him), and then Tony burst into tears. Of course, we were all crying. It's just the saddest thing I've ever experienced in my entire life.

But I guess I needed to go and be with the others. Somehow it's comforting to be with people who are in the same kind of pain. Andrea and I hugged and cried for a long time (I think we both felt like sinners who deserved to die far more than someone as good as Clay). All the youth group kids were there, and we went into another room separate from the adults for a while. Zach sort of acted as the leader and no one complained. Beanie was there too, and I could tell she'd been crying a lot, but I hadn't talked to her since earlier today when she and Zach dropped me home from school.

All the McFadden kids filled us in on all the horrible details of the shooting (some of them had witnessed the entire horrifying event). It was more details than I ever wanted to hear. But I think they needed to talk about the whole thing—sort of get it out of their systems, I guess. We are all in shock over it still, and we all miss Clay more than words will ever say. For a long time we sat there remembering all the things he had said to us in the last few weeks.

Then Andrea spoke up and said, "It's kind of like when Jesus died, isn't it?" We all knew what she meant. I mean, it's probably sacrilegious or something to make that kind of comparison, but we couldn't help it. Clay was so good.

Then I said, stupidly enough, "The only problem is that Clay won't rise from the dead in three days."

But Zach challenged me on that. "He has already risen from the dead," he said as if he personally knew something we didn't. "Right now, Clay is in heaven with Jesus." Several others agreed. I suppose they're right, but all I could think was, a whole lot of good that does me. I wanted him to be down here where we could see him and listen to him.

About then Tony came in and asked if he could have a short word with us. I felt so sorry for him—he looked so tired and sad. But his words didn't sound tired and sad. And he proceeded to tell us about a Clay we had never even known.

As it turns out, Tony and Clay moved here a couple years ago (after Tony's wife had died of cancer). Before that Tony had been a pastor in a big city, where he had raised Clay after his parents had died when Clay was only ten. But apparently after Judith (Tony's wife) died, Clay had started getting really rebellious and getting into all kinds of trouble—serious things like drugs and stealing and all sorts of stuff. I know everyone in the youth group was totally shocked to hear this; I guess we had begun to think that Clay was just about perfect. Anyway, Tony said he wasn't telling us this to in any way diminish Clay's memory, but so that we could all see how far God had taken Clay in a very short time.

After getting arrested (at only sixteen), Clay hit absolute rock bottom and finally called out on God, and then he rededicated his life to Jesus. "And it was like night and day," said Tony. "We moved here, and I've never seen a life change so completely, so quickly—it was a real miracle." He sobbed as he continued. "God gave Clay two amazing years and I know Clay is sitting next to Jesus right now—and he's having no regrets."

Then Tony just totally broke down and we all went up

and hugged him and told him how much we loved Clay and how much his life had meant to us, and how thankful we were to have known him—even if it was only just briefly.

Now I'm sitting here thinking, maybe that's just the way it is. We all have a certain number of days to live, and we don't know the number. But at least Clay was living his life to the best of his ability. And, like Tony says, I know he has no regrets.

Then I wonder, could I have said the same if I'd been killed in a drunken driving accident last weekend? Not hardly. It's a lot to consider and I'm not even sure what I think about everything yet. But I don't think I'm mad at God anymore. For one thing, I know that would make Clay sad. And, no, I'm not living my life for Clay. But I just don't want his life to have been wasted on me.

There was a message on our answering machine from Josh when we got home tonight. But I just can't bring myself to call him back. I just don't think I want to talk to him yet. Zach is going to drop Beanie by to spend the night here. I think she is taking this even harder than me. I'm not sure why. But I suppose I'll find out; we'll probably talk about this all night.

May 14, Monday

We had a very moving memorial service for Clay in church yesterday; the room was packed with people I've never seen there before. The youth group had offered to sing the song that Clay had written (and sung to us

just a week ago—I cannot believe it was only a week; it
seems like a hundred years!).

We practiced most of the day yesterday until we got
it almost perfect. And I think everyone appreciated it.
Then Tony talked about Clay's life (some of the same
things he'd already told us) and then he spoke about
the seed that falls to the ground and dies and then a
hundred new plants spring out of it. He said that just last
night God had showed him that that's how it would be
with Clay's life. And something inside of me agreed.

Today there was a burial service at the cemetery
for Clay and even more people came (several hundred, I'm
sure!). The cars were lined up for about a mile, and I
think almost every kid from McFadden plus a bunch from
Harrison were there too (including Josh). They even had to
set up a PA system so that everyone could hear. And we
sang Clay's song again—I still can't sing it without crying.

It was a good service, and I know many people were
deeply touched. And although I'll never, ever get over losing Clay, I feel like I can keep going now. Like, for Clay's
sake, I want to love and obey God more than I've ever
done before. And today, for the first time since Friday, I
felt this little twinge of, I don't know, almost like joy—but
not real bubbly or anything. Maybe it was more like
peace; I'm not sure. But anyway, it was a good twinge.
Kind of like a deep sigh. And I felt like everything is going
to be okay after all. I'm still pretty sad too. Hard to
describe, I guess.

Afterwards, Josh came up and gave me a hug and

wanted to give me a ride home. But I said, "No, I need to ride home with my parents," which wasn't exactly true (I mean they weren't making me), but I needed to because I wanted to. I've felt closer than ever to my family these past few days (even Benjamin!), and I don't mind spending time with them. I know it's been like that for a lot of the kids in our youth group. And I think it's a good thing. A lot of us were getting sort of wild and pushing our limits and stuff. Maybe this was a good reminder that family is important.

But I do feel sorry for Beanie. She seemed so confused the other night. Her mom isn't doing so well, not that that's anything new (Lynn has a new boyfriend who sounds like a major creep), and I know Beanie has been depending on Zach for a lot (too much I think). So, anyway, I said to Beanie that I'm here for her. And that I plan on being a whole lot more available, and maybe we both just needed to give this boyfriend thing a rest for a while.

I don't know if she took me too seriously (or maybe she thought I was just saying all that to be nice), but I really did mean it. I even told her if she needed a place to stay, I could probably talk my parents into letting her come live with us. And I'm pretty sure that I could. My parents really seem to be changing since they're back together and going to Faith Fellowship. It seems like their relationship with God is becoming more real too. Right now, in spite of all the tragedy, I feel just slightly hopeful about a lot of things.

But one thing I'm not too hopeful for—it's me and Josh. I just don't know what to do about that. Right now, I don't even want to think about it.

EIGHTEEN

May 17, Thursday

It's been a pretty quiet week in our town, sort of like someone spread a thick gray blanket of sadness over the whole place. I think almost everyone is grieving in one way or another—even the grocery store has a black wreath hanging by the front door. The other two funerals were held this week, along with a big memorial service at McFadden High last night. Their school won't open their doors until the middle of next week. The other kids who were shot have been released from the hospital now and it sounds like they're all making fairly good recoveries—many people attribute this to all the prayers that have been going up all over town (and even across the country!).

It turns out that the other two kids who died in the shooting were both Christians. In fact, they were friends of Clay (we just learned that this week). And Pastor Tony's "seed" theory is really proving to be right on the money, because lots of kids have been giving their hearts to Jesus throughout the week. Everyone is talking about it. And I must admit it's encouraging to see such things. (Still, my heart aches for missing Clay.) But I do think it would make him happy to see everything that's happening as a result (and maybe he's up there watching).

All those national media vans have finally disappeared from hanging all over town, and I think life is slowly returning to a subdued sort of normal. I suppose in time our town will fully recover, but I doubt if we'll ever forget. I know I'll never forget. So far there doesn't seem to be any big explanation for the kid who did the killing; I mean, other than he was really angry and had access to firearms. Some kids say he belongs to some satanic internet group, and he took a vow to kill Christians. But all kinds of rumors are floating around right now, and I'm not sure what's true and what's not, but time will tell, I guess. Pastor Tony says we all need to keep praying for him, no matter what he's involved in—and that that's what Clay would want. So, I try, but I must admit my prayers sound a little halfhearted to me. But maybe God understands.

May 18. Friday (what to do?)

Okay, here's what's bugging me today. (I know it sounds pretty silly and insignificant after everything else that's happened in the last week, but it's a problem just the same.) You see, my parents both seem to really like Josh (he's been coming by our house more often lately), and even Benjamin seems to think he's okay, especially when they shoot hoops together. And I know my mom is thinking it's so wonderful that I'm going to the prom with him and all. So now I'm wondering, what in the world am I going to do about all this?

I mean—I do feel like I'm supposed to break up with him, but how will I explain this to everyone? And what if they're all disappointed and everything? Maybe I should just wait until <u>after</u> the prom (well, not the very next day, of course, but a week or so after). But then it'll be graduation time (for Josh, I mean), and I know there'll be all sorts of parties and stuff where he'll want to have his girlfriend along with him to celebrate. And, well, I just don't know what to do about this whole stupid thing! To be honest, going to the prom still sounds like fun (maybe not as great as it used to sound, but it'd probably be fun).

On top of everything, my mom wants to go looking for a prom dress with me tomorrow (and I know she's really excited about all this—almost like we're planning a big wedding or something). I just feel so totally torn. I mean, ever since Clay's death, I've gotten closer than ever with my parents, but I've also been getting closer and closer to God. And I'm really starting to believe that my relationship with Josh has been a hindrance to my relationship with Jesus all along (just consider the way we started out!). I guess I almost feel (as Clay used to say) "convicted" about this whole thing. Clay told us once how God had given him certain convictions and at the time I wasn't totally sure what he meant by that. Except that he said it was a personal thing and it was different for everyone. But he said that when you got one <u>you knew it</u>.

Well, I think I've got one and I'm pretty sure that I know it. I'm just not totally certain how to handle it without hurting a whole bunch of people and making a great big mess of everything. But I do have a feeling if I wait too long, it'll be even worse, and maybe too late.

DEAR GOD, PLEASE HELP ME TO KNOW HOW TO HANDLE THIS. I THINK YOU'RE TELLING ME TO BREAK UP WITH JOSH. BUT A BIG PART OF ME IS STRUGGLING WITH IT. PLEASE, SHOW ME SOMEHOW WHAT I NEED TO DO. THANK YOU.

May 19, Saturday (Mom comes through)

I wimped out and went ahead and shopped for prom dresses with my mom today. After trying on about a hundred gorgeous gowns I just burst into tears. Well, my mom told the salesclerk we'd be back later, and then she rushed me out of there and into a nearby deli, where she ordered us both turkey sandwiches (thinking I was suffering from low blood sugar or some such thing). Anyway, I couldn't stop crying. And about then she decides I must still be grieving for Clay (which may actually be true) so she very sweetly tries to comfort me by saying how we all loved him, but we need to move on with our lives and things like that. By then I just can't stand it anymore, so I blurt out, "I can't keep dating Josh."

Well, my mom sort of blinks in surprise, and then asks me what exactly is going on. And I cannot believe it, but I sit right there in the corner booth of The Great Tomato Delicatessen and tell her almost everything that has gone on with me and Josh. And she listens, then simply says, "Well, honey, if you need to break up with him, you better do it right away."

I felt so incredibly relieved, it was like I'd been being squeezed in a giant vice and suddenly someone took off the pressure. I asked if she was disappointed that I wouldn't be going to the prom, and she just laughed and said, "I'd rather see you happy than going to dozens of proms, Caitlin. Don't you know that?"

And I must confess that I didn't. I always thought Mom wanted me to be really popular, a cheerleader, and maybe even the prom queen. I told her thanks for every-thing and we hugged. I think it's one of those mother-daughter moments that I'll always remember—<u>and</u> we didn't even have to buy a silly dress either!

So, here comes the hard part. It was time to call Josh (for some reason it didn't bother me to call him for this). And I tell him that I need to break up with him. He doesn't question it or anything. He just says, "Okay," and then hangs up! Just like that. Well, I guess I should be relieved that it was so easy, but it kind of bugs me that he didn't even want to talk to me about it, or try to convince me otherwise, or anything! To be totally honest, his apathetic response kind of hurt my pride. I mean, it's not like I wanted him to come crawling on his knees to me, but it might've been nice to see just a little regret on his part. After all, he does have a little something to do with me wanting to break up—he did act like a complete jerk more than once. But then, I need to remember, this con-viction came from God not Josh.

And now, I've obeyed God. And actually considering I just gave up going to the prom with one of the cutest guys in school, I don't even feel that bad. In fact, I really feel relieved. And free. I know this sounds weird, but somehow I think Clay is up there cheering for me right now. Anyway, I know that God is! And that's what really matters.

May 20, Sunday (public confession)

For some reason I wanted to share the story of my first real live conviction with my youth group at church today. I guess it's because we've gotten so close to each other since losing Clay. Anyway, I went ahead and told them all about it (well, not everything). But, I think it meant something to several of them. Andrea came up to me afterwards and actually thanked me for sharing. She said it gave her something to think about. But Beanie acted kind of funny about it. After church she asked me (privately) "Does that mean you think you're better than Zach and me?"

I was surprised, but said, "No, not at all. The stuff between me and Josh was definitely one big mess. It was hurting me a lot, and I know that's why God wanted me to break it off with him. Like Clay said, a conviction from God is an individual thing."

I don't know if she really understood what I meant or not, but I figured she'd have to sort it all out for herself anyway. I did tell her if she wanted to hear more about this, I'd be happy to tell her the reasons I had to break up (I'm not terribly proud of everything that went on between me and Josh, but I'd be glad to share if it'd help her at all). Still, she didn't seem that interested. So, I just hugged her and told her I loved her. We've all been doing a lot more hugging lately—since losing Clay.

And our youth group has really grown—from about a dozen to almost fifty! And now a college guy named Greg Thiessen has stepped in to lead our group. He's really nice and everything, but not the same as Clay.

May 25, Friday (outside looking in)

It's been a pretty lousy week for me. All anyone can talk about these days is the prom (which happens to be tomorrow night). And even though it was my choice not to go, I feel totally out of it right now. The good thing is I'm really relying on God to help me through this whole thing. And I've felt spiritually stronger than ever before in my entire life. Still, I'd be a big fat liar if I said that everything is just great. It's hard being an outsider. At the same time, it makes me wonder how Jesus might have felt sometimes. And maybe Clay too. Then suddenly I feel stronger, like everything's going to be okay, and that this is all for the best in the long run. Still, it's not easy.

It sure didn't help to see how quickly Jenny and Josh got back together (I guess I should've known). It seemed like this week turned into a mad scramble of everyone changing dates with everyone else. (Totally weird, if you ask me, and did I mention a little shallow? Of course, only recently I was equally shallow so I better not judge!) So without going into all the pitiful details, I think everyone is finally all settled with who's taking whom to the prom. And somewhere (way down in the high school clique system) there must be a surprised girl (who never thought she had a chance) who is now going to the prom with some poor guy whose date bailed on him at the last minute just to go with some more popular guy. So I guess at least one person is happy. Actually, so am I. It's just a more quiet sort of happy.

I kind of wish I had something fun to do tomorrow night, but on the other hand, what if I suddenly got all depressed and down and didn't want to be around anyone right at that moment. I'll pray about it, and maybe God will give me some ideas. Just in case, I'm making this all seem like some big horrible, awful thing, <u>it's not</u>. The enormous relief I feel inside of me far outweighs what I may (or may not) have passed up.

Furthermore, I've recently heard all this chatter about how all the guys are reserving hotel rooms and I suddenly realize exactly what Josh's expectations might have been for me <u>after</u> the prom—and I'm sitting here thinking: <u>Thank God for sparing me from that</u>. I'll be praying especially hard for Beanie and Zach. I'm not sure where they are right now regarding all this (and I believe Clay's death had an effect on that part of their relationship), but I also know Beanie's been awfully unhappy lately, and I just wish I could help.

NINETEEN

May 26, Saturday (proms, prayers, and promises)

Here I sit, alone, in my room. Oh, woe is me. (NOT REALLY!) Actually, I'm kind of enjoying the solitude.

My family went to dinner and a movie tonight. And after about twenty minutes of begging and pleading for me to join them, they finally gave up when I somehow managed to convince them that 1) I am not depressed, 2) I am not suicidal, and 3) I just want to be alone. That's really all there is to it. I just wanted some time to think and to pray.

It's been a totally beautiful spring day today with blue sky, sunshine, birds singing in the trees—perfect day for a prom. That's really okay, it's not like I wanted it to rain or anything. Mostly, I just want for that whole thing to be over with so I won't have to think about it anymore. Before long, the seniors will graduate (including Josh, thank goodness) and then school will be out for the summer. I can't wait! My dad says I might be able to get a job at the ad agency (they're looking for someone to help the receptionist) and I just might look into it. Also, our youth group is planning a two week mission trip down to Mexico this summer. It's an idea that Clay had come up with last winter (and I have to admit that no one was very interested at first, but now they've really into it).

I guess because he's gone, we're thinking differently about things like reaching out to others, and maybe we'll do it in his memory—sort of a tribute to his life. It won't be until the end of August, and the purpose is to build houses for poor people and at the same time tell them about Jesus. It's sounding pretty good to me, and I really hope I can get a job and earn enough money to go. Anyway, I'm really looking forward to seeing the end of this school year. Not that it's been all bad. I mean, it's sure been different and everything (nothing like I had expected when we started classes last fall). I guess if I had the whole thing to do over I wouldn't do it all that much differently (and that even includes Josh, because I actually think I may have learned some important lessons with him).

So, I've been sitting here getting philosophical about the stuff that's happened in my life lately. I've also been doing some praying, as well as reading my Bible. I know, it probably sounds like I'm becoming a real fanatic religious freak, which I am not. But I am falling more in love with Jesus all the time. I can't even explain it, but I know that it's very real—and it's pretty cool.

And suddenly I'm hit with this really radical, and somewhat awesome, idea. I think it's coming from God. But before I write down another word about it, I want to take some time to really pray and consider what's going on here. I just want to make sure I'm really hearing God's voice speaking to me, and not my own. Although I seriously doubt that I'd come up with an idea like <u>this</u> by myself. No, I'm pretty sure this is a God thing (Clay used to use that little phrase a lot).

(Later the same night)

So anyway, I went outside for a while and I just walked around the neighborhood, enjoying the soft twilight (the sun had just set and the western horizon was glowing all rosy and pink, and the eastern sky looked like a smooth piece of smoky blue velveteen rolling out). Anyway, I was just walking and praying and thinking about this idea that has just hit me, and finally I decided <u>this must be of God</u>. And for that reason I'm going to act on it. I guess I'd have to call this another conviction (my second one so far) although it kind of seems like something more than that too. I guess it's like a conviction with a commitment attached to it.

It has occurred to me today that it's definitely God's will for me to remain a virgin until the day I marry (that is <u>if</u> I ever marry—and who knows?). And so, on this day (May 26) I am making a vow to God to totally abstain from having sex until my wedding day. I know some girls have made these really public vows about this very same thing, but somehow (to me, anyway) it seems like this should be a very private moment between a person and God (not that I won't share this with anyone who wants to know) but for me it seems more special to make this promise with only me and God present—and then to record it in writing in my diary (just in case I should ever forget, which I'm sure I never, never will!).

SO, RIGHT NOW, I PROMISE YOU, ALMIGHTY GOD, THAT I WILL REMAIN FAITHFUL TO THIS COMMITMENT. I WILL NOT HAVE SEX AND I WILL REMAIN A VIRGIN UNTIL MY WEDDING DAY (IF THERE EVER IS ONE). I TRULY BELIEVE THIS IS SOMETHING YOU HAVE LED ME TO DO. AND I THANK YOU FOR LOVING ME ENOUGH TO DIRECT ME LIKE THIS. MY HEART AND MY BODY BELONG TO YOU, DEAR LORD. AMEN.

(even later that night)

Okay, I'm really glad I did this, and this is a day I think I will always remember (almost as significant as the day I invited Jesus into my heart). I guess I should be thankful I kept a diary this year—I mean, some of the best moments of my life lie within these very pages (yes, and I suppose some of the worst are here too).

But I'm not stupid, and I have no doubts that keeping this kind of a commitment won't be easy (especially when it seems that just about everyone I know has had, or is having, sex these days). But with God's help I'm sure I can keep my promise. Which brings me to the second part of this whole thing. While I was walking around my neighborhood, it occurred to me that dating really puts a girl in some pretty compromising situations (well, guys too, I guess). It seems to me that once you're out on a date and all alone with a guy (especially someone you feel really romantic about) it's only natural that you end up kissing, and then, of course, one thing easily leads to another. And before you know what's happened, temptation is furiously beating on your door, and everything just turns into one great, big mess.

So, I think the only thing for me to do is to seriously consider giving up dating altogether. I have to admit that I'm not totally positive about this decision yet—and I can't even say for sure that this is a real conviction from God (not like my vow to remain a virgin), but I do know that I'm seriously concerned as to whether dating is a very healthy thing for me to participate in, just now anyway. I mean, I suppose it's possible that some girls can date guys without having these problems (although I can't think of a single one offhand), but I think for me, it might simply be best to quit dating completely, at least for the time being. Man, wouldn't my dad be totally shocked?

Just for the record, I still want to go out and do things with groups and friends and stuff like that. And to be honest, I'm not even totally sure how I define dating, but I think it's like when Josh and I spent time alone by ourselves, and things <u>always</u> seemed to get carried away. Like I said, I'm not totally sure about all this yet, and it might take some time to figure things out and see how everything plays out. But I do think it's a step in the right direction for me, and I feel pretty good about it. And it does go well with my promise to remain a virgin.

I think the hardest part of all this will be trying to explain it to others. I mean, I don't want anyone to think I've become a nun or anything (I mean, I'm not even Catholic!). But take someone like Beanie for instance—I'm sure she'll think I've totally gone off the deep end here. Maybe it'll be best not to mention it to <u>her</u> right now. I'm not sure, but I think God will show me in time. One thing I'm certain of, Clay would have understood all of this, and he would've appreciated it too. In fact, I'm sure it's a lot like the commitment he made to God about not having a girlfriend. I didn't understand it at all when he told us about it. But I do now. Totally. But I'm not just making this commitment because of Clay; his life and death have certainly had a huge impact on me, but the commitments I've made tonight are about <u>me and God</u>— and that's pretty much it.

GOD, HELP ME NOW TO KEEP THESE COMMITMENTS TO YOU. I KNOW WHERE I AM WEAKEST, AND I ADMIT TO YOU THAT I'M REALLY AFRAID THAT I WILL FAIL. THIS IS A BIG STEP FOR ME—I REALLY, REALLY NEED YOUR HELP! AMEN.

TWENTY

May 27, Sunday (a new friend)

I had a really great day today. Youth group
was good with lots of people sharing amazing things that
God's been doing in their lives just recently. It's really
cool—kind of like God is just pouring himself out over all of
us! It made us wonder if Clay's not up there right now
asking God to take special care of us. Whatever it is, it's
absolutely fantastic!

I even felt like it was okay to share with the group
about last night's commitment to God (I felt slightly self-
conscious, but I think I needed to say it out loud—kind of
like a public confession or something), and anyway I know
there were a couple kids in there who were <u>really</u> listening and thinking about the whole thing (including Andrea
LeMarsh). Beanie and Zach weren't there today (probably stayed up too late with the prom and all), but maybe
that's why I felt more free to share. Not that I won't tell
Beanie about this; I just don't want her to take it all
wrong, like I'm judging her or something—because I'm <u>not.</u> I

mean, it's not hard to understand why she's decided that having sex is okay. For one thing she is totally in love with Zach (and I have to admit, he seems a lot more thoughtful and mature than Josh in some ways). But add to that how Beanie's mom never seems to care about what she does; and then look at the example that Lynn sets in her own life. So, you see, I'm really not judging Beanie. I just don't want to see her get hurt, is all. And I admit I'm worried about her.

Anyway, after youth group, Andrea invited me to go to the mall with her. We had fun hanging out together. I've discovered there's a lot more to this girl than meets the eye. I must admit that when I first met her, I thought she was (let's see, what's the right word) haughty maybe. I think it might just be because she has really good posture (which she informs me is due to many years of ballet lessons). She's actually quite pretty, but she doesn't dress in the latest fashion, and her hair is long and usually pulled back in a long ponytail. I guess she's what you'd call a classic. Kind of like Audrey Hepburn (and I just love old Audrey Hepburn movies).

Even though Andrea and I are quite different, we seem to get along just fine. And I think that's because of God. Andrea told me today that ever since Clay died, she's been getting closer to God too. She'd been really struggling with everything before that (like, remember the time I saw her at that drinking party, and she was acting sort of snooty). Well, it turns out she was in a situation very similar to mine, only the guy she was dating didn't even call himself a Christian. So, anyway, she's broken it off with him too. But she told me today that she is still a virgin. Now, I must admit that surprised me because I was feeling like I might be the only one left and something of an oddity. She said that all her friends at McFadden thought she was sleeping with her old boyfriend, but that for some reason she had never done it. Now she's really relieved that she didn't and is seriously considering making the exact same commitment to God that I did last night.

I told her that this decision was between her and God, but that I was really, really glad that I'd done it. I mean, it just makes me feel so free and totally at ease (and it takes the pressure off) to realize that I don't have to struggle with those questions anymore. I feel like I'll be able to focus even more on the things that really do matter, like God, for instance, and friends, and even school! Andrea she said she's going to pray about it. And she said if she does follow through on this that maybe we can start a little club (she was joking, I think, but who knows?). Maybe it's not such a bad idea after all.

May 29, Tuesday (making plans)

Today there was a lot of talk about the prom and all the happenings connected with it. Interestingly enough, several couples seemed to be having some "technical difficulties"—including Josh and Jenny. She was really in a snit about something today (and she didn't seem to be talking to Josh at all). I can't help but wonder...although I really <u>don't</u> want to hear about it. Anyway, she and I still talk occasionally, and sometimes I think if Josh had never come into the picture (or if Jenny wasn't so wrapped up with her popular friends) we might still be friends. Or maybe not. But, anyway, I try to be nice to her. And I think she appreciates that.

At track practice (this is our last week before district), I noticed that Josh seemed to be hanging around me a bit. I know, it might just be my imagination. It's not like he and I don't talk anymore, because we do exchange a chilly but civilized greeting upon occasion (which is more than enough for me, thank you very much!). But for some reason he seemed to be lurking around the high jump pit a lot today. Coach Reynolds told me to only concentrate on high jumping for this upcoming meet (since my long jump hasn't been too spectacular lately). And the high jump pit is on the other end of the field, so I don't know why Josh kept hanging around. But if he thinks there's any chance of us getting back together, I'd be happy to set him straight—and fast! Oh, I wouldn't be rude, but I'd make it very, very clear.

That's another reason I'm so glad about the commitment I made to God, otherwise I might find an opportunity like this quite tempting. And now it's really not. Okay, maybe just a little... But because I've already made this decision, it's almost like I don't really have to deal with it that much. It just kind of frees me up. Anyway, after practicing for about an hour I left school and went over to my dad's office (Mom let me use her car today). I

went to the ad agency to apply for that job Dad had
mentioned last week. It felt kind of funny being there
(after the last time when I found out about Belinda,
who, I've since heard through Aunt Steph, has thankfully
moved away). I wore an outfit that looked pretty grown
up and mature and I carefully filled out my application
(with my best printing) and then had a quick interview
with the receptionist. She seems pretty nice, and says
she has too much to do and needs some part-time help.
Then she sent me up to talk to the personnel director,
which gave me hope—like maybe I passed the first test.
Anyway, I'll know in about a week. I prayed about the
whole thing and decided not to worry about it.

   Aunt Steph said if I didn't get a job there, she'd be
glad to hire me to baby-sit Oliver during the summer, but
I think I'd rather flip burgers or pump gas. (Not that Oliver
is so bad—he's actually kind of sweet—but I've spent
enough other summers baby-sitting, and I'd like to move
up a little now). Still, if that was my only way to make
enough money to go on the Mexico trip, I'd probably do it
just the same.

   While I'm on the subject of Aunt Steph, I must mention
this latest little development (which Steph says is
absolutely nothing, but I'm not so sure). It seems that
Pastor Tony stopped by her work last week and invited
her to lunch. Now Steph swears that he does this with
lots of people in the congregation, but I'm not totally convinced. After all, I've seen him playing with Oliver after
church, and well, you just never know. But I'm thinking

isn't it just totally amazing to consider where Stephie was only a year ago, and where she is now. It's mind-boggling. But God could do something like that. I'm sure of it!

I didn't see Beanie at school or even at track practice today. Zach was there but not talking much; I think he's concentrating on this upcoming meet (he wants to qualify for state). So I called Beanie at home tonight, but her mom said she didn't know where she was. Then I prayed for her. I feel worried that something may be wrong.

May 30, Wednesday (trouble brewing?)

I'm pretty sure that Beanie is either avoiding me or that something is troubling her. I saw her at school this morning and called out, but she just kept walking, looking at her feet as she went. Then I didn't see her anywhere at lunch, but I spotted Zach and went to see if he knew what was up. He told me that they'd agreed to spend a little less time together until he finished up track season. It's important for him to do his best because he has a good chance of getting a college sports scholarship out of it.

But then after school, Beanie didn't even show up for track practice again, and Coach Reynolds asked me what was up with her. I said I didn't know, but he said now that she's missed three practices she can't compete in the meet on Friday. Somehow I don't think she'll really care. I tried to call her again tonight, but this time no one answered. I left a message, but I doubt that she'll call me. I think the next time I see her I better just go tackle her or something. I really do miss her. I suppose she's just down in the dumps because she and Zach are cooling it for the time being, but I think it's understandable. I know a college scholarship is really important to him. And I'd think that Beanie would understand that too. Then again, I know how insecure she is; she might be taking this too hard.

May 31, Thursday (poor Beanie)

I finally cornered Beanie and demanded that she talk to me. She reluctantly agreed to see me tonight, and I went over to her house after dinner (since she refused to leave; I think she expected Zach to call or something—which he did not). Anyway, her house was a mess (as usual), or perhaps worse than usual because Beanie usually straightens it when she thinks someone's coming over—it was apparent she didn't clean it for me (and her mother never, and I mean _never_, cleans it up).

   Her mom wasn't home tonight so we sat in their tiny kitchen (amid the squalor which was pretty disgusting) and I asked Beanie what was up. She just shrugged and said nothing. So I persisted. I told her I knew something was wrong, and I was pretty sure it had to do with Zach, and that since I thought I was still her best friend (even though I blew it a few months last winter) that she owed me some kind of explanation for the chill treatment she'd been giving me lately. Then she began to cry. I don't just mean quiet tears; I mean horrible, gut-wrenching, heaving sobs.

I felt so horrible. In the first place, Beanie is (and always has been) one of the toughest girls I know. In middle school she got beat up once, by three girls who said they were in a gang, and she never even shed a tear. But now there she was, sitting at their messy little plastic-topped kitchen table, just literally crying her eyes out. And I didn't know what to do. So I just sat there watching dumbly and praying silently. I finally got up and searched for a slightly clean glass and filled it with water, set it in front of her, then wrapped my arms around her and held her while she cried some more. I think I was crying then too, although I wasn't even sure why, except that my friend was hurting. Finally, she stopped and began to take little sips of the water. Still I waited. And then she told me.

Beanie is afraid that she is pregnant. Oh man, I did not know what to say to that. I just sat there in shock, wondering what in the world a seventeen-year-old girl does when she's pregnant. I mean, both Beanie and I are hugely opposed to abortion (we even participated in a Right to Life parade once in middle school). So anyway, I didn't know what to say. Finally I asked if her mother knew. She said no. Then I asked if Zach knew (of course I know Zach must be the father). But again she said no. That's when I realized I was the first person she'd told this to. Poor Beanie—what a huge load to carry all alone. So, I asked her if she'd taken a pregnancy test or anything, and she said she was too scared to, but that she thought she had all the typical symptoms (like upset stomach and, of course, missing her period).

Well, it was just too much to take in, but I think that silent prayer must've worked and that God was helping me to speak because the next thing I said was, "Beanie, it doesn't matter if you're pregnant; God still loves you and so do I. And even though you're feeling so miserable right now, I just know that good is going to come out of this somehow. And no matter what, I'm going to stand by you and be your friend. Do you understand that?" She nodded. Then I said, "I know Zach will stand by you too. He's a good guy." Again she nodded and we hugged.

She told me that the reason she hadn't mentioned it to Zach was so he could focus on his track—and hopefully make it to state. "That means you can't tell him for two weeks," I said. "How will you manage to keep it from him that long?" She wasn't sure, but she was determined she would. Right then I think I admired Beanie more than ever. I mean, here she was suffering (and it had as much to do with Zach as her) and yet, in a way she was protecting him so that he could do his best in track. I asked her what her mom would think, and again she just shrugged. "Who knows?" she finally said. "You can never tell. She might just pretend like it's nothing, or she might go through the roof."

Suddenly, I just wanted to rescue Beanie from all this. I mean, she and I have always talked about how we'll get an apartment together when we're out of school. But I wondered if she could even last that long. And that's when I thought of Aunt Steph (as well as her need for a baby-sitter).

So, I told Beanie I had this idea; it might not work, but it was worth a try. Then I called Aunt Steph and just basically told her the whole story. Now some people would be put off hearing about a high school girl getting pregnant and everything, but Aunt Steph was so cool about it. Without even pausing, she said, "Why doesn't Beanie just come live with me for a while? If she likes it and wants to baby-sit Oliver during summer, then great. And if not, we'll just part as friends. Do you think she'd like that?" I wished I could've hugged Aunt Steph right over the phone, but I told her I'd check with Beanie and call her right back.

Well, to make a long story short, I helped Beanie pack her stuff, waited while she wrote her mom a note, then drove her over to Steph's place. I know it's not such a big thing, but somehow I think it encouraged Beanie, and Steph seemed really glad to help out. Even if it's just for a little while, it might give Beanie some time to think and to sort out her life. And I know Steph is a good influence right now (not to mention understanding).

So tonight I'm going to bed with very mixed feelings: 1) I'm terribly upset and worried about Beanie, but 2) I think she's in good hands with Steph, and 3) I just hope I can keep my mouth shut where Zach is concerned, at least until track season is over.

And, not that I'm gloating (because I most certainly am not) but at the same time I am so enormously thankful that God showed me how much I needed to make that vow to him—and I do realize that I could very easily be in Beanie's shoes, and I thank God I am not. Just the same, I mean what I said tonight: I will definitely stick by her through it all. No matter what.

TWENTY-ONE

June 1, Friday (district meet)

I placed third in high jump today (not too bad, all things considered). After my event was finished I hung with Beanie who was being brave and cheering Zach on, who, by the way, outdid himself. Zach took first in two races and second in one. Poor Josh didn't even place. I was glad for Zach (although at the same time slightly perturbed that Beanie was bearing her troubles alone). But when Zach wanted to take us out to celebrate, I started to decline until I saw the pleading look in Beanie's eyes and realized that this was part of standing by her, and so I agreed.

Now if I had realized that meant Josh was joining us too, I might have said forget it. Not that we were having a date (at least not in my mind), but it felt a little like it just the same since I had to sit in back with Josh. But instead of getting all worked up, I just turned and asked him what Jenny was doing tonight. He made a glum face and said they were'nt getting along too well just now, and that he didn't know why he'd ever gotten back together with her (which I hoped wasn't a lame try to regain my affections!). Just the same, I didn't make any more inquiries, but instead tried to focus my attention on Zach and how well he'd run his races today. I think that made Beanie happy, and somehow I managed to survive our little celebration dinner.

Then Beanie came over to spend the night at my house (she's asleep already; I think being pregnant makes you really tired). But we stayed up pretty late talking too. She said her mother didn't call to check on her last night, so she figures she doesn't care and is probably glad to be rid of her. I just can't imagine how that would feel if my mom wanted to be rid of me. Poor Beanie, and just when she could really use a mother's love. Apparently it went okay with Aunt Steph last night. We'll see how it goes. Beanie used to dislike Aunt Steph, but she's watched her change in the last six months and I think she's appreciating her more than ever. And Beanie said she'd really like to baby-sit Oliver this summer, and how that will help get her used to being around babies. When she said that I felt a chill of shock run through me as I remembered again that by next year, Beanie would have a real, live baby! It's almost too weird to even think about. And I have a hard time talking about it with her. But maybe that's where Aunt Steph will come in handy. I still haven't told Beanie about my virginity vow to God. I kind of think that would be just about the last thing she needs to hear right now. Poor Beanie.

June 3, Sunday (just an ordinary day)

We had a car wash after youth group today. Both Beanie and Zach participated and everyone was getting all excited about how fun it will be to go to Mexico together and everything. Then I glanced over at Beanie to see this really sad look in her eyes, like her life (or maybe just her youth) was all over with now. And I wondered if being pregnant means she shouldn't go to Mexico (would it hurt the baby or something?). It's still just so much to take in.

Afterwards a bunch of us, including Andrea, went out for burgers and Andrea started to jokingly mention something about "our vows" but I managed to stop her and change the subject. I just didn't want Beanie to hear about that yet. I wondered if there was some way to warn Andrea off without totally spilling the beans. I guess I'll be relieved when the state meet is over and Beanie can finally tell Zach. Until then, my lips are sealed (as are Aunt Steph's). Speaking of Aunt Steph, Beanie and I observed her chatting with Pastor Tony (a little longer than seemed necessary). I'm wondering if there really might be something to my suspicions, and now with Beanie staying with Steph, we'll have a built in spy (not that we're spying), but I do think it'd be cool if Steph and Tony really hit it off, and I sure wouldn't mind having Tony for an uncle. He's had so many sad things in his life—and

Steph is really a lot of fun. Anyway, I'll keep praying for them (to discover God's will in this regard), and I'm sure God can work out all the details.

June 5, Tuesday (now what?)

Okay, this takes the weirdness award of the week (as far as I'm concerned). Tonight, who shows up on my doorstep but Josh Miller! Well, I don't want to be impolite or anything, but I want to know why he came. Of course, the next thing I know, dear Benjamin is dribbling a basketball all over the driveway, loudly begging Josh to play Horse, and, of course, Josh agrees. So I go in the house thinking, Fine, he came over to play with my little brother. Mom looks at me kind of funny, and I quickly explain that I did NOT invite him over, nor am I pleased that he's here.

Well, my dad overhears part of our conversation and speaks up (in what I'm sure he thinks is a very fatherly way). "Sounds like you're being kind of hard on poor Josh, Catie." I look to my mom for help and she just makes a funny face. (I never did tell my dad about why I broke it off with Josh, and now I suspect my mom didn't either—which she probably thought was what I wanted at the time.)

So I lamely say to my dad, "But I don't really like him, Dad."

Then my dad kind of laughs and says. "Well, maybe you need to give the poor guy a second chance. You know we men can make mistakes sometimes." I want to say,

Okay, who are you and what have you done with my dad? but by then Josh is being led through the back door by Ben who is getting him a soda. I just roll my eyes at Dad then go out to see how I can best get rid of Josh.

Finally I get Josh out to the front porch (a few steps closer to his Jeep) and I ask him, point blank, why he came over here. Big mistake! He immediately starts doing this song-and-dance routine (did I mention well rehearsed?) about how much he cares for me, how he's missed me, how I've hurt him. And finally, just when I'm afraid that I'm starting to fall for it (and I can hardly believe what a wimp I am!), I hold up both hands and tell him to stop, that I don't want to hear it.

Then I say, "I'm sorry if I hurt you when I broke up, although you seemed to recover pretty quickly by getting back with Jenny—" Of course he cuts me off there, saying how it was Jenny who came after him (which I can believe by the way). But anyway, then I realize I HAVE to tell him about my vow to God, and for some reason I find this awfully embarrassing. But my heart starts to pound and then it's as if Jesus is standing right by my side, saying, "Go ahead and tell him everything." Well, I haven't even told my parents yet, and the windows to our house are all open, and somehow I just don't want them to over-hear our conversation like this.

So, I ask if we take a ride. And he grins big and says, "Sure." And I'm certain he thinks he's gotten through to me (and who knows what else he thinks on this warm sum-mer evening). So we start to drive and I immediately tell him (in surprising detail) all about my vow to remain a virgin and how I may not even date anymore. Well, at first he thinks I'm kidding, but I assure him I'm dead serious. Then he just gets real quiet. And finally he says, "Does this mean you're going to become a nun or something?"

Which makes me laugh, and I have to admit I was worried people would think that. But I tell him, "No. It's just something I believe God wants me to do—to protect me. And since I made this vow I've been really happy and relieved. And I plan on sticking to it." So he asks what's wrong with dating, and I have to explain that it just puts me in a situation where I might mess up on my vow and I don't want to do it. Then an idea hits me (you see my grandma in Pasadena is a recovering alcoholic). So I say, "It's like an alcoholic who's made the choice not to drink anymore—she wouldn't want to spend any time hanging out at the bar, would she?"

Anyway, he got my point and started to take me back home. Then I said something I never dreamed I'd hear myself saying to Josh Miller. "You know, I really do like you, Josh. And when I was first getting to know you, do you remember how we were just friends. Remember how we talked in the library and stuff?" He nodded.

Then I said, "I'd still like to be friends with you like that."

He laughed. "It's never supposed to be good news when a girl says she 'just wants to be friends with you.'"

I shook my head and said, "But this is different, Josh. Just being friends is a really good thing!" Then I stuck out my hand and we shook to friendship, and Josh made me promise not to tell any of his buddies about this.

And once it was all said and done, it was kind of a nice relief to have a chance to say those things to him. Sort of like no hard feelings, you know. And, who knows, maybe Josh will grow up in time and turn into a strong Christian, and then who knows? But, believe me, I am not holding my breath. And this will not, (in any way, shape, or form) change or affect my vow to God.

Now I get the feeling that I'll have to tell my parents about this whole thing, and I'm just not sure how to go about it. I mean, it's not like you just announce to everyone at the dinner table, "Hey, everyone, I've decided not to have sex until I get married!" No, I'm sure there must be a better way. I guess I'll just have to ask God to show me when and how to best do it.

TWENTY-TWO

June 8, Friday

Only one more week of school. And tomorrow is the state track meet (not that I qualified). But Mom said I can borrow her car to drive Beanie and me up there. Mom's been a whole lot nicer to Beanie lately. I think it's because she suspects there's something seriously wrong between Beanie and her mom (which has resulted in her moving in with Steph). And, since everyone knows Beanie's mom is sort of messed up, naturally Mom's sympathy would lie with Beanie. I'm just not sure what Mom will say when she discovers what's really going on with Beanie (and thankfully, Steph isn't saying anything just yet). So far, it's going really well with Beanie and Steph (Beanie's been watching Oliver a lot for her, and she actually seems to really like the little rug rat— maybe something maternal has kicked in with her). It's a relief having Beanie in a safe place. I was afraid she was about ready to lose it, and I think Steph is good medicine.

I still can't believe that Beanie has managed to keep her secret from Zach. I don't know if I'd have that much self-control—I think I'd want the guy to suffer with me (not that I'll ever get in <u>that</u> situation). I suppose Beanie had plenty of practice keeping her mouth shut when she lived with her mom. Sometimes I thought that was why she was so crazy and outspoken in other circles. But she sure hasn't been like that lately. She's like a totally different Beanie. Mostly she's quiet and introspective these days. And sad. <u>Very sad.</u>

I'm afraid to ask her what she plans to do about school next year. I mean, some girls go to school while they're pregnant, but I've seen them getting teased a lot too. And Beanie has so much pride, I can't imagine her handling that very well. I suppose she's so smart she could just take her GED test and be done with high school altogether. But that seems kind of dismal and <u>anticli-mactic</u> (there you go, Miss Tyler, my new vocabulary word for the day—and it means something like a letdown). I think it would be a big letdown to miss your senior year. I mean, I've always looked forward to being seniors together with Beanie (sort of ruling the school, you know).

But who knows, maybe she doesn't care about that kind of stuff anymore. Maybe she's thinking about being a mom, or perhaps something as crazy as marrying Zach!! But if she and Zach did get married, how would they

ever go to college? And, good grief, she's only seventeen!!
But I'm sure it would be really hard to give up your baby
for adoption. And I know she'd never consider abortion—it
goes against all she believes about the sanctity of life
and everything. On the other hand, she was always
thinking about the sanctity of other people's lives, and
now, it's her life that we're talking about here. Oh, man,
too many things to consider—just way too confusing for
me. I'm glad I'm not making these kinds of decisions. Best
to keep praying for her—that God will show her what to
do. For now I'll just stand by her and continue to be her
best friend.

Speaking of friends, I actually had a nice chat with
Josh at lunch today. No pressure or anything, just a normal
friendly conversation. I kind of think he liked it too. He
and Jenny are still broken up and I notice she was looking
our way; I wanted to reassure her that I was absolutely
no competition. And who knows, maybe someday I'll even
tell her what's up with me. Although I doubt that she'd
understand (she's not even a Christian), but it might just
make her think. For all I know God could be working on her
even as I write this. Anyway, she's on my prayer list, which
is getting quite long by the way.

June 9, Saturday (winners and losers)

What mixed feelings I'm having after the track meet
today. First off let me say that Zach was totally incredible
out there! In top form, he beat his own personal best time in
every race—and placed first in two races and third in

one. We were just going nuts in the grandstands for him.
Beanie was so totally proud of him, she was literally beam-
ing (the first time I've seen her look happy in weeks!).

Afterwards we headed down there to congratulate
him, and we noticed that an older guy, wearing a polo
shirt from a prestigious and private (out of state) college,
was talking to Zach. So we just stood off to the side and
waited. Then he finally left, and we ran over to hug
Zach, and that's when he told us that the guy was the
college track coach and he was offering him a full athletic scholarship. Zach was so thrilled. (His parents can't
afford anything but community college to start out with
and so this is a really huge deal for him—everything he's
been working for and dreaming of for a long time.)

So, Beanie congratulated him and acted like that
was just great, but I could tell she was hurting inside. I
congratulated him too, and then he told us that Coach
Reynolds was taking him out for dinner to celebrate, and
that he'd see us both at youth group tomorrow.

I'm not sure if Beanie had even planned on telling him
right after the meet, but I guess it was kind of her to
allow him a chance to enjoy his achievement for a while.
He'd be brought back down to earth soon enough anyway. But then on our way back home, she announces
that she's not going to break the news to him until after
graduation. Well, in my opinion, that's going way above and
beyond the call of duty—and so I tell her. And, of course,
we get into this big old fight over the whole thing. And
she tells me not to try to run her life. As if!

What I couldn't make her understand is that I'm only thinking of her own welfare. This is just too huge of a burden for her to bear all by herself. I mean, didn't Zach have something to do with making this baby? It only seems fair that he should suffer a little too. But Beanie wouldn't hear of it, and she made me promise to continue my vow of silence. So I just continued it all the way home!

Honestly, times like that with her, and I just totally lose my patience about everything. I suppose she's right—I would like to tell her how to live. I even wanted to tell her that if she hadn't had sex with Zach in the first place she wouldn't be in this position right now. But I'm so glad I had decided to keep my mouth shut just then. After I cooled off, I realized how that would have been really cruel on my part. Because who am I to say whether she should tell him now or not; maybe there's a good reason for her to wait until he graduates. I just hope (when he finds out) that he'll appreciate everything she's gone through for him!

June 12, Tuesday (my future's so bright I need sunglasses)

The seniors have flown the coop. They don't come to class all this week, and so everything seems kind of quiet and flat around here without them. I hope it'll be better than this next fall when we're the seniors (although I still don't know if Beanie will be here then, which makes me wonder if I need to be on the lookout for a new best

friend). Of course, Beanie and I made up over our silly
fight in the car the other day. And now that she and
Zach are spending more time together again, she seems
a little happier (which makes it easier to get along with
her).

The good news this week is that I got the job as a
part-time receptionist at the ad agency (no burger flip-
ping for me!). I think it'll be fun acting like a grown-up and
wearing office clothes. It's only five hours a day, but hey,
that means I can sleep in during the mornings. And for
two weeks in July I'll work full-time while the regular
receptionist takes her vacation time. I already told her
about my Mexico plans, and she said it'll be fine, and
that their company has even been known to donate
towards certain charitable causes! So life is looking up
for me right now.

Beanie has agreed to baby-sit all summer for Oliver. I
feel kind of sorry for her (since she used to hate baby-
sitting in the past), but maybe this is helping her realize
what being a full-time mommy is all about. She still hasn't
told me about what she plans to do. I guess it'll all
depend on what Zach says after graduation. What a
shock that's going to be! I mean, I can just imagine Beanie
shaking his hand after he gets his diploma and then saying, "Congratulations on graduating, and oh, by the way,
you're going to be a daddy." Not that she'd do it like
that. But can you imagine? I mean, what if Zach fainted
from shock or something? Anyway, I'll just be really glad
when this whole thing is out in the open.

Speaking of out in the open, I told my mom about my vow yesterday. We had gone to the mall to get a birthday present for my dad (it's his birthday this weekend). The timing just seemed right, so I told her. She was really sweet about the whole thing (actually, I'm sure she was probably relieved). She asked some questions, and then told me that she thought I was turning into a "very wise and mature" young woman, and that she was surprised I hadn't been bugging them for a car lately.

Well, in an effort of extreme self-control (not leaping out of my chair), I said that I thought having a car could be very helpful to get me to and from work, but that I also knew I could ride the bus to get there. She smiled at that (probably saw right through me). Then I mentioned that I might make enough money to afford a small car payment each month (and still have enough for the Mexico trip and hopefully some school clothes in the fall). I told her I'd seen an ad on TV recently (at Price's Auto Mart) where you could "drive away a car for as little as $99 a month," but I wasn't sure if that would really be much of a car or not. And she said, she didn't know, but maybe we could check it out!

So, now I'm imagining myself behind the wheel of a blue (or maybe yellow) VW Bug (you know, with the bud vase on the dash). But I suppose that might be dreaming a little too big just now, and maybe a little shallow too. At least it seems possible that I might get some wheels! I can't wait to tell Beanie.

June 13, Wednesday (another happy surprise)

Okay, I'll admit it, I'm the type of person who has occasionally daydreamed about standing in the limelight (I mean who hasn't?). Like I had actually hoped that I'd make it to the state meet in high jump, but coming in third at district just didn't quite cut it. I suppose for a brief time, I even entertained illusions of being crowned prom queen along with Josh as king. (By the way, that honor went to Nathan and Heather, _not_ Josh and Jenny like everyone had expected!) And I'll admit that I sometimes think it would be fun to actually be someone like Gwyneth Paltrow and have your face on the cover of lots of magazines. Yes, I'm certainly no candidate for sainthood yet, and I definitely do lean toward shallowness sometimes (although I'm battling against it).

So, anyway, you can imagine how thrilled I was at the awards ceremony today when Miss Tyler announced that I had won the state creative writing contest (I didn't even know I'd been entered!). It was actually kind of cool to walk up there (amid the applause) and claim my award (a nice plaque with my name on it) along with a two hundred dollar savings bond that goes toward college tuition—and, here's the very best part, my short story will be published in a national teen literary magazine within the next year. So for the rest of the day, I felt like I was sort of floating. I even called both my parents at work (leaving a complete message so they wouldn't get all worried and think I was in the hospital or something).

Then when I got home, my mom had actually put together a special celebration dinner with crepe paper and balloons (she didn't actually cook, but had stopped by for takeout Chinese with all my favorite dishes).

So, there you have it, you get up and go to school, thinking it's just another ordinary day and the next thing you know, something totally unexpected happens! Life's like that. I guess it's like Forrest Gump said about the box of chocolates—you just never know what you're going to get!

Beanie was really sweet about the award, congratulating me and everything, but I couldn't help wondering how she was feeling underneath it all. I mean, she's really the academic (although her grades don't always show it) but I think her relationship with Zach (this spring) might have distracted her from her schoolwork worse than usual. And believe me, I know how that can happen. She's usually the one who wins an academic award now and then, and here she doesn't get a single thing today! Not only that, this could very well be her last year of school. Oh, it's just too sad to even think about!

TWENTY-THREE

June 15, Friday (Harrison seniors graduate)

Josh actually invited me to go to the graduation all-night party with him (but just as friends, he said). I really did think about it, but finally decided it was a bad idea. I didn't tell him it was mostly because I don't trust myself. I'm afraid that if I spent all that time with him (even with a bunch of other people around) that I'd start wanting him as my boyfriend again, and as a result I could be putting my vow at risk. And in the end, it's just not worth it. He said he understood and that he respected that I was sticking by my promise to God. I think he even meant it. He's really interested in our Mexico mission. Zach had told him a little about it, and I guess Josh is even considering coming along too. Of course, I wonder if Zach will actually go once he finds out that Beanie's pregnant.

Speaking of which, she didn't break the news to him the minute he received his diploma (so there was no fainting on the gym floor). I doubt that she'll even tell him tonight since they're going to the all-night party together. I've decided that's her business anyway, and I'm sure she'll tell him when the time is right.

I cried at graduation. I'm sure everyone thought it was just because I was sad to see all the seniors moving on, but the real reason was that I was thinking about Clay and how he would have graduated from McFadden (they hold their ceremony tomorrow); and anyway it just got to me. Of course, a lot of people cry at graduations, so it's not like I really stood out or anything. Then I noticed that Beanie was crying too. I'm not sure if she was crying for Zach, or maybe Clay, or perhaps it was just the harsh realization that she might not get to do this next year. I don't know, and I didn't want to ask.

Anyway, I left Beanie there with Zach (I had given her a ride) and then I went on home. And I suppose I felt just slightly bad that I'd turned down the invitation to the all-night party. I mean, it sort of feels like I'm on the outside looking in again. And I'd be a liar to say that doesn't hurt just a little. Okay, for a moment there it hurt a lot!

But the thing is, I'm doing what I believe God wants me to do, and that fills my heart with a certain satisfaction that is bigger and better than going to any kind of party. And so, I'm really okay with everything.

Aunt Steph was here when I got home. It seems she is

going to go with Pastor Tony to the McFadden graduation tomorrow night (which she said is _not_ a date!). I guess Tony is going to say a few words on behalf of Clay, and he wanted someone along for moral support and asked her to join him. She invited me to come along too. I told her how I'd sobbed at tonight's graduation (just thinking of Clay) and how I might totally go to pieces tomorrow. She said that was okay, she expected there'd be a lot of tears. I could tell she wanted to ask me about Beanie and Zach. I know (like me) she wishes that Beanie would just get it all out in the open. But my parents were around, so we couldn't discuss it. I expect she'll hear something from Beanie before I do though.

June 16, Saturday (a very somber graduation)

I went with Tony and Steph to the McFadden graduation. We sat with a bunch of kids from the youth group. I felt kind of sorry for the actual graduates (although at least they're alive) because it seemed that so much attention was focused on the two seniors who weren't there. It was a pretty somber ceremony. Andrea LeMarsh told me that the senior class had decided that their graduation should honor the memory of Clay and Brittany (the other senior girl who was killed and who would have been valedictorian). Her brother got up and said a few things on her behalf, and then some of her friends did too. Then Tony spoke about Clay. Well, all I can say is, I'm sure there wasn't a dry eye in the entire house. But the strange thing was, I felt better when it was all over. Maybe it was just another step in the grieving process, but I think we all felt like we'd moved one more step towards healing.

Afterwards, we went out for pizza with a bunch of the youth group kids from McFadden (who weren't seniors or going to their all-night party) and then we went and played miniature golf until eleven o'clock. It was actually a lot of fun, and we all acted pretty goofy. Zach and Beanie weren't there. And when I asked Steph if she'd heard anything, she just shook her head and said that Beanie had slept most of the day (probably worn out after the all-night party), so I'm guessing that Zach doesn't know yet.

Tomorrow's my dad's birthday, and we're having a surprise birthday party for him. I'm supposed to get him out of the house under the guise of car shopping (my idea, of course). But I also plan to give him my "gift" while we're out. It's not actually a real gift; I made him a card with a special poem that I wrote for him (I know, just because I won that writing award, there's no stopping me). Anyway, this is the poem (it's pretty corny, but I know my dad'll like it):

Daddy's Little Girl
by Caitlin O'Conner

Remember how I used to hold your hand
Long ago when I was quite small.

But still you call me Daddy's Little Girl
Even though I have grown very tall.
There were times when we did not agree
When all we did was argue and to fight
About silly things like boys and going out
And dates that lasted way into the night
But Daddy's Little Girl is growing up
And starting to see things the way you see
And suddenly I've come to realize
That what you do, you do since you love me!

Then I signed the card and wrote down the date "May 26"—but I didn't explain why. I'm hoping he'll ask and then I'll tell him about my promise to God, and then I'll tell him about how I'm not really into dating right now. Which I'm sure he should appreciate seeing how last winter he was so totally opposed. I figure his recent change of heart (like when he was pressuring me to go out with Josh) is only because he's trying to show that he trusts me now, which is actually rather sweet. But I want him to understand my decision and why I made it so he can be supportive of it. Besides, like Mom, I'm sure he'll be relieved. Especially when they learn the sad news about Beanie.

Now I just hope that Dad doesn't think I'm trying to soften him up just so that I can get a car (although it's not such a bad strategy, come to think of it, but it really wasn't my original intent!).

June 17, Sunday (Dad's birthday surprise)

Well, I took Dad out car shopping (as planned). After we'd looked at a couple of lots, I asked him if we could go sit down and have a Coke. So then while we're sitting at a picnic table outside this greasy little burger joint next to the car lot, I give Dad his card (and although it wasn't a Hallmark, it was certainly a Hallmark moment!). Naturally, my dad got kind of teary-eyed. Then he thanked me and said he'd treasure it always, and we talked a little about all the stuff that went on this year, the good and the bad. And he said, once again, how much he regretted that whole thing with Belinda, but did I know that I played a crucial part in keeping him from proceeding any further in his relationship with her?

I said, "No, how was that? All I remembered at the time was acting like a spoiled brat." He smiled and said that it all started with that day I showed up at his office, just before Valentine's Day. Then he proceeded to tell me how Mrs. Greenly mentioned my stopping by, and how I'd waited in his office for a while, and then how I'd left rather suddenly and looked sort of upset. Well, I was pretty surprised because I hadn't even known that he'd been aware that I was there.

"Furthermore," he continued and I could see he was still slightly uncomfortable or maybe just embarrassed. "When I looked in a certain drawer, I could tell that you'd seen it—the card had gotten caught in the drawer and was bent." I almost said I was sorry, but realized that would be silly. Then he told me that he never did give her that bracelet, and that he had returned it later that week. He had bought it while flirting with the idea of having an affair. And although he continued seeing her off and on (for lunches and dinner), it just never went further than that.

"So you see," he said as he reached for my hand, "I think God sent you as my guardian angel that day." Well, I never would've guessed that my visit could have made any difference. But here's the funny thing—after the shock of discovering about Belinda, I can't even remember why I went there in the first place. I know I'd been upset about something, but that's about all I remember.

Then my dad asked me what the date May 26 meant—was that when I'd written the poem? And so I told him. Then he really did cry. I felt sort of bad, making him cry like that on his birthday, but then I remembered how much better I felt after crying for Clay again last night. I even told Dad all about that. Then suddenly I looked at my watch and realized it was time to head back to the party. Dad couldn't understand why I didn't want to keep looking at cars, but I told him we could do it another day (which I'm hoping he won't forget!).

The party was a success. Dad was totally surprised. Benjamin had been in charge of decorations which explained the really wild selection of colors and about a thousand balloons all over the place, which we all ended up popping before the night was over.

Beanie and Zach were there too, and I could tell by

the tightness around Beanie's jaw, and by Zach's happy disposition, that she had still not told him. I even took her aside at one point, and without being too pushy encouraged her to take care of this business. She assured me that she planned to. Although I have my doubts. And Beanie's so thin, that I can just imagine her stomach starting to stick out before too long, and she'll probably just tell Zach that she's been putting on a little weight! Come on, Beanie, just get it over with!

TWENTY-FOUR

June 21, Thursday (last day of school)

School at long last is over, and not a moment too soon as far as I'm concerned! The only teacher I was slightly sad to say good-bye to was Miss Tyler, because she's not coming back next fall. She's getting married and moving to Hawaii of all places (can't feel too sorry for her about that). Anyway I gave her a card and thanked her for being such a good teacher, and she said she expected to read one of my books one day! I'm not taking that too seriously, but it was really nice just the same.

Beanie informed me today (after me not bugging her all this week—what self-control!) that she plans to tell Zach _tonight_. He's taking her out to dinner to celebrate the last day of school. He already got a summer job with the parks and recreation (working with little kids, no less—great preparation for fatherhood I suppose). Anyway,

I made Beanie promise to call me tomorrow morning to tell me everything. And I promised to pray for her while she finally breaks the news. Man, I don't think I could even take it much longer! I almost said something to Mom just yesterday when she wanted to know if Beanie would be able to go on the Mexico trip too.

This weekend, Dad's going to take me car shopping again. I think we've got it narrowed down to a second-hand car (three or four years old and hopefully not ugly); it has to be something safe and get good gas mileage. Dad tried to talk me into a small pickup that he could borrow sometimes, but I flat out refused—that is, unless <u>he</u> wants to pay for the whole thing (in that case I just might consider it).

I also told my parents that I won't mind continuing to work part-time during the school year (so I can make my car payments), but they told me it was too soon to decide, and they were more concerned with my education than about my financial contributions. But a lot of seniors do go to school for part of the day and then work the rest. And since I haven't lost any credits (although I came close last winter), I can probably do that. But, like my dad said, I'll think about that later. For now I just want to enjoy a few carefree days of summer. I don't start work until next Wednesday.

June 22. Friday (a friend in need)

I waited until noon for Beanie to call, then finally broke down and called her. But no one answered, which is

strange because I thought she was going to start baby-
sitting Oliver today. Then Steph called me and asked if
I knew where Beanie was; it seemed she never came
home last night. Now, this has me worried, so I call Zach's
house, but his mom says he's working today and she hasn't
seen Beanie (and the way she says it, I can tell she must
not like Beanie very much and that bugs me).

So, I think I'll try Beanie's mom, but I can't imagine
why Beanie would go there. Unless, perhaps, she wanted
to tell her about the pregnancy. But surely, she wouldn't
have spent the night. So I call and there's no answer. Now,
I'm feeling kind of freaked and really wishing I had a
car. Mom's still at work (teachers have today to clean up
and stuff).

So, I hop on my old bike and ride over to the park
where I think Beanie said Zach is supposed to be working.
And sure enough there he is with a bunch of little kids
hanging around. It's kind of a sweet scene, but I'm really
not in the mood to appreciate it. Anyway, I walk up and
ask if he knows where Beanie is. Well, he looks real surprised to see me, and I can tell by the look on his face
that he knows. But I don't want to say anything about it
right now. Then he tells me that she wanted to be
dropped off at her mom's last night. That's the last he
saw of her.

Now I'm getting all worried, thinking Beanie has told
her mom and her mom has flipped out and like killed her
or something. Now, I know that sounds like overreacting on
my part, but I've seen Beanie's mom lose her temper

before, and it's pretty scary. Something like this could really set her off. So by the time I get to Beanie's mom's house, my legs are actually shaking with fear. Thankfully, her mom's old beater car isn't in the driveway, so at least I won't have to face her. But after I knock on the door for a long time, no one answers and I'm thinking, what if Beanie is in there all beat up and unable to answer the door? Or what if she's dead? I don't know what to do. I consider breaking in, but if there's nothing wrong here, I could get into a lot of trouble (Beanie's mom is just the kind of person who might actually press charges!). So I consider calling the police, but what would I tell them?

I bang on the door again, this time I'm yelling out Beanie's name, certain that the neighbors will be over here any minute, but then at least I can tell them that I'm worried for my friend's safety. And then, finally, just when I think I'm about to totally lose it, the door opens, and there stands Beanie looking like she really is half dead.

"Are you okay?" I ask and she just shrugs then walks away and sinks into the disgusting heap in the living room that they call a couch. So then I lash into her (my fear has turned into anger) and I ask her what she thinks she's doing, not coming home to Steph's place, not telling anyone where she is, and how worried I've been.

She just looks up at me and tells me I'm not her mother and that I should get a life. Well, that really makes me mad. But instead of really letting her have it,

I just look at her. And suddenly I see just how hopeless her life must seem to her. And suddenly I just begin to cry. I tell her how sorry I am, and what a lousy friend I am, and how I'm just so relieved that she's okay. Then she begins to cry too. And we both just sit there crying. Then I ask her if we can go outside in the sunshine and get some fresh air (it's really bad in the house—I think it's gotten worse after Beanie left).

So, we sit out on her dilapidated porch and she tells me the whole story about Zach. Of course, he wasn't too happy to learn that he was going to become a father— what eighteen-year-old guy with a bright future is? I guess he even blamed Beanie for it at first. (Although according to her, he's the one who was using "protection," which she has since learned isn't a hundred percent fool-proof—DUH!) So anyway, Zach finally reassures her that everything will be okay, and that he'll take care of her. She said it was the first time in weeks that she felt like she could actually breathe.

Apparently her relief was short lived, because then Zach said he had an aunt who worked for Planned Parenthood, and she knew all there was to know about getting an abortion, and that she might even know how they could get some financing help too. Well, Beanie just came unglued at that point. And since they were down-town (not too far from where her mom lives) she started to walk home. Well, Zach wouldn't let her walk, but he brought her here. And that was that.

Thankfully, Beanie had the clarity of mind (amazing,

after all that went down last night) not to tell her
mother about the pregnancy. She said her mom was
actually in a pretty good mood (and not drunk). But
after they talked for a while, Beanie just went to bed. I
felt sorry for Beanie having to sleep in there. So then I
asked Beanie what she planned to do (I actually just
meant for the day, like did she need a ride over to
Steph's place) but apparently she thought I meant her
whole life in general.

So she emphatically informed she would not have an
abortion—ever, no matter what! And that she planned to
give the baby up for adoption because she didn't want
to end up like her mom (poor and a single parent). And
that after the baby is born (which she figures will be
just after New Year's—I hadn't realized it would be that
soon!) she will get a job and try to continue her schooling
part time. I nodded, trying not to show how pitiful this
whole thing sounded to me. I mean, at least she has a
plan, I'm thinking. And then she sort of laughs and says,
"Oh, yeah, that's if I don't kill myself first."

Well, I'm hoping she's kidding, but I'm not too sure. So I
remind her that to kill herself was as bad as an abortion
(actually worse!) because she'd be taking an innocent
life with her. She looked at me funny, but at least I think
it made her think. Then I suggested we walk over to my
house which is about a mile away, because it was nice
out and not too hot. And I knew she was probably hungry.

Then after I fixed her a nice big lunch, she took a
nap. And that's where she is right now. I already called

Steph to tell her everything was okay (well, sort of) but I'm not calling Zach. I don't mind if he worries a little about her. At least, I hope he will. Zach has gone way down in my opinion today. I guess I shouldn't be so hard on him. But I thought all Christians believed that abortion was wrong. I guess I was mistaken.

So much for my first relaxing day of summer vacation!

June 23, Saturday (an amazing story)

Tonight, Beanie and I had dinner at Steph's house. Beanie and I cooked. Then after we got little Oliver to bed, we all sat and talked about everything. Steph acted really gracious toward Zach's position on abortion, saying that not so long ago she thought a woman's "right to choose" was the only way to go too. And that only recently had she begun to seriously question these things herself. That was mainly the result of their Bible study group (led by Tony).

It seems that Tony had told them all the story of how his mother had gotten pregnant with Clay when she was almost forty, and both parents worked hard just to keep food on the table for the other three kids. Anyway, the mom decided to get an abortion. Tony was a sophomore in high school at the time (the oldest of the kids and the only one who knew she was pregnant) and she asked him to drive her to the clinic. So all the way to the clinic, he questioned her decision and pleaded with her to reconsider. Finally, Tony begged her not to abort the baby, and actually promised that he would take care of the baby himself. Well, his mom was so shocked that a sixteen-year-old boy could care so much that she changed her mind—and that is how Clay came into the world!

And throughout high school, Tony helped with his little baby brother as much as he could, but by then the mom was glad she'd had the child. And then when Tony's parents died in a car accident about ten years later, Tony, barely out of seminary, but true to his original promise, took in his brother and cared for him ever since. Tony's point, obviously, was that there was a divine purpose to Clay's life (even if it did seem short-lived to us) and that no human person should ever try to play God by deciding who should live or die.

I told Steph that maybe Tony should share that story with Zach, and Beanie strongly agreed, so Steph is going to talk to Tony about it on Sunday. In the meantime, Beanie doesn't plan to talk to Zach. She said she needs some time and space to think about her relationship with him.

June 24, Sunday (a special day)

Zach didn't come to youth group today, and Beanie feels like it's all her fault. I told Beanie that it was Zach's choice, and she couldn't blame herself for that. I encouraged her to focus her attention on her relationship with God, and not to worry about Zach. I wanted to say more, but didn't want to sound like I was preaching. Besides, there's a verse in Proverbs about just a few words being better than many. Hopefully, Beanie will begin to get things right between her and God—because if ever anyone needed help and direction in her life, I'd say Beanie Jacobs should be at the top of God's list. I know she's at the top of my prayer list.

After church, Dad and I went car looking while Ben and Mom went to get him some new cleats for baseball—his feet have gotten bigger than Dad's (and smell ten times worse too!). Anyway, after we'd looked at about a dozen cars (none of which seemed just right), Dad suggested we take a break and get a Coke. It's a funny thing, but we ended up at the same greasy burger joint as on Dad's birthday.

But today is lots hotter, and we sit in the shade sipping our drinks as I tell Dad that I don't want to drive a car that looks just like Grandma's (that seems to be the one he's got his eye on). Well, he just laughs and says he understands, and maybe we can do better. Then he reaches in his pocket and pulls out a little box and hands it to me. So, I'm wondering, what's the deal—my birthday isn't until August. Then I think, could there be a key in here, did Dad already buy my car? (I hope not, because I know for a fact it would be a Ford Taurus because "they're so safe.")

When I open it, it's a small gold locket. Very pretty. "What's this for?" I ask. Then he says to open it. Well, instead of a spot for pictures, it has a place where it's engraved with May 26 with a cross beneath it, and then my name on the other side. And, of course, I know exactly what this means. Dad smiles and says, "I just thought you should have something to commemorate this special day." I don't know quite what to say (I don't ever remember my dad being this thoughtful before!), so I just thank him and put it on.

We didn't find the right car today, but that's okay. What I brought home was a whole lot better!

Before I go to bed tonight, I'm thinking how thankful I am for both my parents, but that makes me feel guilty because I know not everyone is as fortunate (and I'm thinking mainly of Beanie). So I am praying specifically for her that she will allow God to become like her father— her Daddy. Because there's a verse about how God is a father to the fatherless (and that pretty much describes Beanie). And I think, even though my earthly dad is pretty cool, he's <u>nothing</u> compared to God. Then I almost feel jealous (but not really) because I realize how close Beanie could get to God if she'd only just do it. And so I'm praying that God will become her Father, and let her know just how much he truly loves her.

TWENTY-FIVE

June 27, Wednesday (first day on the job)

First of all, I got my very first car on Monday night. Okay, so it's not a VW Bug. But at least it's not an old lady car either, and it's even kind of sporty with five gears (and already I'm pretty good at shifting). It's a three-year-old Plymouth Breeze (just enough bigger than a Neon that my dad thought it would be safe, and it also gets really good gas mileage). The first thing I did was to go pick up Beanie and take her for a joy ride. I could tell she was a little jealous (and who can blame her with all the things she has to deal with), and so I decided to tell her how I've been praying for her (that she'll realize that she's really God's very own daughter, and how not having an earthly father can be really special because it makes God watch out for you even better).

She kind of frowned at first and then said, "So far, it doesn't seem to be working out all that well." So I told her that had more to do with her choices than God's. And I challenged her to live like she was really and truly God's own special child and to just see what happened. And then, with a serious expression, she asked if I was planning to go to seminary and become a lady preacher or something—to which I just laughed. Me a preacher? Now that's pretty funny.

She said that Tony had made a date to take Zach out for dinner on Friday night, and she thought he was going to tell him the story about his mom. I told her I'd be praying for Zach to, as Jesus says, "have ears to hear." She said she'd be praying too.

So, today I went in to work at ten o'clock, and man, there's so much to learn, and I feel so totally stupid. I connected several callers to the wrong people, got names mixed up, and all kinds of things. I can't believe Rita (that's the receptionist) didn't just fire me on the spot. Who would've thought just answering the stupid phone could be so hard. But I told her I'm going to try really hard, and maybe by next week she can actually take a coffee break without freaking out that I'll blow up her entire switchboard.

Dad came by while I was working (and I know I looked all flustered) but he just winked and gave me a thumbs-up sign. Then finally it was time to go home, and I was so relieved. I prayed all the way home that God would help me to get the hang of things before Rita decides to give up on me completely. I'm sure she can't believe that Mike O'Conner's daughter is such a total dunce!

June 29, Friday (hoping for a miracle)

Well, I think it's a miracle, but I'm finally getting the hang of things at work. I only made about five mistakes today (compared with about a hundred the day before). Rita says I'm going to be just fine. I'm not telling her that I had a nightmare about her being gone on vacation and me just totally blowing it. I have three weeks before she leaves. Maybe I'll be ready. I'll keep praying

Speaking of praying, tonight was the night Zach went to dinner with Tony. Man, was I praying for him. Beanie told me that Zach had really been pressuring her this week to get an abortion. She said his aunt said it's best to do it in the first trimester (and she's almost in the second). Then Zach said that as the father he had the right to say she should get an abortion, because otherwise that meant that he would have to support a dependent against his will, which seems totally ridiculous if you ask me. But Beanie said she's pretty sure that his aunt is filling him full of stupid ideas, and that she has no intention of keeping the baby or making Zach support her against his will.

But here's the really cool news. Beanie said that she's been praying to God as if she really believes he's her Father, and that she's really starting to feel differently towards him. She's realizing how many mistakes she's made and then blamed God for. And she told me

that she can pray for literally hours at a time. Now, I
could hardly believe that, because I've never prayed
that long. But I don't know why she'd make something like
that up.

And I must admit, she seems different. More peaceful,
for one thing. And also, she has this kind of confidence
about her. But the most noticeable thing is that she kind
of seems to glow. Now, I know that sounds silly, and maybe
it's due to being pregnant. But, honestly, she seems different. I even told her so, and she said that God was changing her from the inside out. She says for the first time,
for as long as she can remember, she actually feels truly
happy. Now, that's amazing! I know if I were in her shoes, I
don't know if I'd be truly happy. But I'm sure glad that
she is.

The best thing she told me, as we drove in my car
with all the windows wide open (pretending we were in a
convertible), was that she had told God that she
wanted to do his will in regard to her relationship with
Zach. And she's decided that if Zach doesn't marry her
(and she's not even sure she wants to marry him) then
she will never have sex with him again.

And that's when I decided to tell her about the
promise I made to God about keeping my virginity. I
thought she would finally understand now. But I think it
kind of brought her down (which wasn't my intention at
all). Because then she said that was something she had
lost and would never, ever have again. Then suddenly I
remembered this Bible verse that Clay used to quote (it

was kind of weird and never totally made sense to me until now); it was about how God can restore "what the worm has eaten and what the locust has destroyed." Now I realize the worm and the locust are like the sin in our lives. So I told this to Beanie and she said, "Do you suppose that God could restore my virginity?" I said, "I don't know for sure. But then God is God, and he can do anything he wants to. I guess it wouldn't hurt to ask." She nodded and said, "Yeah, especially since I know he's my Father now. I think I'll ask him."

Now, to tell you the truth, I think that's a whole lot to ask of God. I know some girls might think that's the easy way to get out of something like losing your virginity or getting pregnant. But let me tell you, Beanie has paid and paid and paid for her mistakes (not to mention some mistakes made by her parents) and if God could make her a virgin again, (and let's just say that he could), I'm all for it. Because, I believe that if Beanie could have it all to do over again, I just feel certain she would do it differently. I've watched her suffer and suffer. And so, for her sake, I really hope that somehow God can restore her virginity. That's what I'm praying for! Besides, God can do miracles—and that would be a real miracle, wouldn't it!

June 30, Saturday (time to close...for now)

It occurs to me that I've been keeping this diary for <u>six whole months</u> now. Wow, I'm actually impressed. And I'm so glad I got all these things down in writing, because otherwise I might not even believe them myself! But I do. And although there were some pretty tough trials and things during the past six months, there have also been a lot of happy times and real victories too.

Now I find that I'm looking forward to the next six months with a joyful anticipation that I didn't even know existed back in January—and all I can say is that it's all due to God. And for that I am truly (from the bottom of my heart) thankful. Oh, believe me, I have no illusions, I'm certain there'll be more hard times ahead—I mean, you just never know what a day might bring. But what I do know is that God can see me through. I can't wait to see what he does next!

a personal note from Caitlin...

Dear Friend,

Do you feel like God is nudging at your heart to make a commitment to him—any sort of commitment? It's best not to put it off, you know. Hey, remember what happened to me?

So, I invite you to sit down right now before God and consider how he may be leading you. Is he asking you to give him your heart today? Is he asking you to dedicate your body to him first and abstain from sex until after marriage? Can you hear his voice speaking to you?

Sometimes it helps to write this kind of promise down. You can do that in your diary like I did, or you can write it down here. Then hide it away if you like, but just don't forget it. Because a promise like this is important—both to you and to God. Because you're his child, and he's always listening.

Blessings!

Caitlin O'Conner

❧ *My Promise to God* ❧

I, _____ *make a vow to God*

                  Print Name Here

on this day _____ *that my heart belongs to him.*

          Print Date Here

And I make a vow to God, with his help, to abstain from sex

until I marry.

         _____

              Your Signature

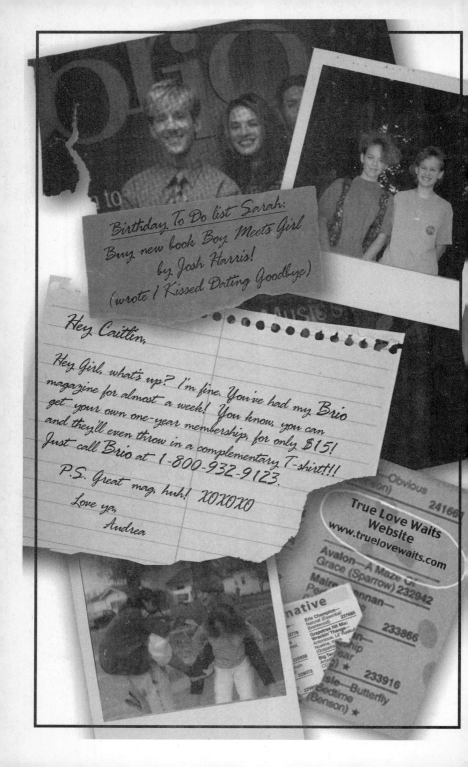

Birthday To Do list Sarah:
Buy new book Boy Meets Girl
by Josh Harris!
(wrote I Kissed Dating Goodbye)

Hey Caitlin,

Hey Girl, what's up? I'm fine. You've had my *Brio*
magazine for almost a week! You know, you can
get your own one-year membership, for only $15!
and they'll even throw in a complementary, T-shirt!!
Just call Brio at 1-800-932-9123.

P.S. Great mag. huh! XOXOXO

Love ya,
Andrea

True Love Waits
Website
www.truelovewaits.com

MORE INSPIRATION

from *Melody Carlson*

Shades of Light

Faced with a dwindling bank account and a heavy heart when her daughter leaves for college, widowed Gwen Sullivan reluctantly takes a job—and discovers hidden talents, self-confidence, and love.
ISBN 1-57673-283-5

Homeward

Fleeing hectic San Francisco, Meg Lancaster returns to the Oregon Coast where she fights to make peace with her family—and discovers love in the process. Winner of the 1998 Rita Award for best inspirational romance novel!
ISBN 1-57673-029-8

Heartland Skies

When her fiancé jilts her, city girl Janie Morgan is stuck in an Eastern Oregon town. Cowboy Harris Anderson teaches her that some men can be trusted in this tender, lighthearted tale of a man, a woman, and a horse.
ISBN 1-57673-264-9